THE BODY IN THE SYNAGOGUE

THE BODY IN THE SYNAGOGUE

RUTI WORRALL

First published in Great Britain in 2025 by
The Book Guild Ltd
Unit E2 Airfield Business Park,
Harrison Road, Market Harborough,
Leicestershire. LE16 7UL
Tel: 0116 2792299
www.bookguild.co.uk
Email: info@bookguild.co.uk

The manufacturer's authorised representative in the EU
for product safety is Authorised Rep Compliance Ltd,
71 Lower Baggot Street, Dublin D02 P593 Ireland (www.arccompliance.com)

Typeset in 10.5pt Adobe Garamond Pro

Printed and bound in Great Britain by CMP UK

ISBN 978 1835742 945

British Library Cataloguing in Publication Data.
A catalogue record for this book is available from the British Library.

This book is dedicated to Ella, Leon and Felix.

CHARACTERS

Chief Inspector Jack Madison
Rabbi Zimmerman
Rachel Zimmerman – rabbi's wife
Mrs Linda Kaufman – wife of Cecil Kaufman
Shiela Roth – Linda's sister
Jane Barker – secretary
Becky Mosco – second secretary
Body – Cecil Kaufman
Sergeant Dave Brodmann
Angi – Brodmann's wife
PC Lisa Thompson
Miki Solomon – ex–musical director of the synagogue
Caretaker – Jon Jonson
PC Benson
Stewart Adams – Jonson's neighbour
Sophie Jonson – Jonson's daughter
Bobby Granger – Jonson's friend
Molly Rubin – member of the synagogue
Sergeant Sean Stewart
Blake Williams – camp owner

1

DAY 1

'Jesus Christ!' Rabbi Zimmerman exclaimed before he choked on his words and glanced behind him, guiltily. Thankfully, he was on his own.

Rachel, his long-suffering wife, had warned him often that the day would come when he would let slip such a profanity from the bimah at the synagogue.

He looked around again, just to make sure. Still no one.

This was a close one. The first time his wife's prophecy had nearly come true.

Which was not really surprising, as this was the first time he had ever come across a dead body on the bimah, sprawled in front of the Torah cupboard. Truth be told, it was the first time he had come upon a dead body, period. Dead people were a huge part of his job but, in general, those would be hidden in a coffin and the rabbi would be spared looking death in the face, so to speak.

Rabbi Zimmerman grew up in San Francisco in a very rich and very secular family. He attended synagogue for a few months, preparing for his bar mitzvah, and never again till he decided to become a rabbi.

What made Ronnie Zimmerman decide to choose the rabbinate as his vocation was not easily understood – not even by Ronnie himself. He initially chose law at university and was set for a brilliant career, following in his father's footsteps. Robert Zimmerman – known as Bobby – was a leading lawyer in San Francisco.

The years at university were wild. Not much time was spent in the library. Ronnie was bright and passed his exams without exerting himself too much, which left him with time for extracurricular activities. Against his father's will – and against all predictions of fame and riches – Ronnie Zimmerman chose human rights law and spent a few years fighting hopeless wars on behalf of his clients.

Miss Barker, who walked into the synagogue hall at that moment, dropped the armful of files she was carrying as she covered her mouth with her hand to stifle a cry.

Having recovered his proper rabbinical language, Rabbi Zimmerman said, 'I think the correct uttering on these occasions is call the police, Miss Barker.'

2

DCI Jack Madison was staring out of the window of his office, pondering his life.

Policing for the last couple of weeks had been slow and dull. There was a pile of papers on his desk needing his attention, but his mind was wandering. He loved his job when things were happening, but the in-between time, that was now stretching a little too long, caused him to question his choice of occupation.

At forty-five, Jack could see fifty around the corner. His jet-black hair was now streaked with the occasional grey which, he was told mostly by females, made him look more distinguished.

Madison preferred it when he was busy on an investigation with no time to overthink things. 'Where am I going with my life?' was a question that only nagged at him when he had too much time on his hands.

Madison had married Lily, his university sweetheart, when he was twenty-seven and she was twenty-five. In those days he did not ponder life. He lived it. They loved each other and the future stretched in front of them in pleasing clarity.

When Lily got pregnant it seemed like the obvious next stage. Home life with children and his beloved wife while continuing to rise up the ranking in his job as a detective was the plan.

But life had other plans.

Lily died in labour and all efforts to save the child failed.

The doctors and everyone he knew told him what bad luck it was. Women no longer died in childbirth.

In a matter of days, he moved from having it all to having nothing and hurting. The pain was such that no medication had been invented that could ease it.

Madison was awakened from his pondering by the sharp ring of the old-fashioned landline on his desk.

He picked up the phone.

'Madison,' he spoke into the receiver.

He listened as the superintendent assigned him to his new investigation.

A body at the local synagogue.

3

DCI Madison and Rabbi Zimmerman stood side by side, looking at the dead body at the foot of the Holy of Holies – the Torah cupboard.

Madison raised his eyes and looked up at the balcony above them.

The rabbi followed Madison's gaze and looked up in the same direction.

'Are you thinking he might have fallen from the balcony up there?' the rabbi asked.

'It is too early to speculate,' the chief inspector answered. 'Was he in the habit of going up in the balcony?'

'Well,' Rabbi Zimmerman replied, 'in the old days the balcony was reserved for the women. These days men and women sit together, mostly down here. The choir sings from up there on special days. High Holidays and the like. Makes them sound like angels.'

Something in the rabbi's voice caught Madison's attention. He shifted his eyes from the balcony and studied the rabbi's face carefully.

'Is that a suggestion that they need to be quite so high to sound angelic?'

The rabbi smiled.

'No. That is not what I meant. They are a very good choir. It is only that referring to the members of the choir as angels is somewhat challenging.'

Madison looked carefully around the synagogue hall. He had never been in a synagogue before and that might suggest that crime was not rife in the Jewish community.

It was a big, airy hall with light streaming in from all directions through the many windows. At one end was a raised section, not high enough to be called a stage, but apparently called bimah – which is, in fact, 'stage' in Hebrew. There was a grand-looking podium at the centre of this section, and the rabbi explained that this was his desk from which he spoke to the congregation. Behind him was a thick, green velvet curtain behind which, the rabbi explained further, lay the books of the Torah (Bible). Above the bimah was the balcony from which, Madison assumed, the dead person jumped; fell; was pushed.

The synagogue hall was filling up with people. White coats galore, policemen, police photographers. The level of noise was attesting the good acoustics of the hall.

'Is there anywhere we can talk, Rabbi?' Madison asked, pointing to the assembled uniforms.

'Sure. My office is just down this corridor.'

Rabbi Zimmerman led the chief inspector to his office.

Disillusioned with his legal career, Ronnie Zimmerman had resigned his job, taken such savings that he had and moved to New York. When asked why he chose New York, he never had an answer. He was running away rather than running to. He did not fancy going somewhere where he would need to learn a new language – and New York was supposed to be a vibrant, exciting place. Young Ronnie thought he needed something different in his life.

DCI Madison looked around the rabbi's office. The shelves mounted on every inch of wall were stacked with books, magazines, some photos and many leaflets and posters. Paper – blank and printed – was everywhere, including the floor.

'I suppose I should apologise for the mess,' the rabbi said, 'but I have given up doing so. Tidiness makes me restless. Besides – I didn't know I was having guests.'

There were only two chairs in the room and one was piled up with books. The rabbi removed the books and motioned the officer to sit down.

'I have to admit, Chief Inspector – is it OK to call you Chief Inspector?'

'It is fine,' Madison said.

'I am two years off retirement, and I really thought I'd seen it all…'

The rabbi left the sentence hanging in the air.

'Sadly, I am not quite so near to retirement, Rabbi, but I can honestly say that a dead body in a synagogue is a first for me too.'

The two men remained silent for a while.

'Are you a coffee connoisseur, Chief Inspector?' Rabbi Zimmerman asked.

This change of subject surprised the chief inspector.

'I beg your pardon?'

'I was about to offer you a cup of coffee,' the rabbi explained, 'but if you are a connoisseur, you would not wish to drink it.'

'Not at the moment, thank you,' Madison replied. He usually carried a flask with his favourite brand of coffee, but did not think it would be proper to bring a flask to a death scene at a synagogue.

'Can I have the full name of the… dead man, Rabbi?'

'Cecil,' answered the rabbi. 'Cecil Kaufman.'

Chief Inspector Madison looked at the rabbi.

'That is an unusual name.'

'For an unusual man,' the rabbi replied.

'In what way unusual, Rabbi?'

'Ronnie.'

'Ronnie? I thought you said Cecil…'

'Please call me Ronnie. Everyone does. There is no need to constantly remind me that I am a rabbi.'

'Ronnie,' the chief inspector repeated. 'What can you tell me about… Cecil?'

'Well,' the rabbi answered. 'He is… was, the chair of the board.' The rabbi hesitated. 'I guess I should say he was, and has been the chair of the board… I mean – when I say he was the chair, you would assume I was using the past tense because the poor guy is dead, but as a matter of fact, before he died, he already was the "has-been" chair. Oh, dear – I don't think I am making a lot of sense.'

Madison allowed a little smile to change his otherwise severe look.

'Let me see if I got it right,' Madison said. 'He used to be the chair but was no longer while he was still alive.'

'Well put, Chief Inspector,' the rabbi replied.

Madison almost invited the rabbi to call him by his first name, but thought better of it. He felt at ease in the rabbi's company and it would be too easy to let down his guard.

'Did Mr Kaufman complete his time as chair? Is that why he was a has-been chair?'

'Not quite. He was voted off only two weeks ago.'

'Voted off?' Madison wondered.

'One usually serves two years in the position of chair. The vote at the end of the first year is normally a fait accompli. No chair was ever kicked off before. The vote normally is a mere formality.'

‘So,’ the chief inspector said after a little pause, ‘I can assume he was not very popular?’

‘He had his supporters,’ the rabbi said, looking uncomfortable.

‘I’m sure he did.’ Madison pressed on. ‘But his supporters wouldn’t have kicked him off the chairmanship, would they?’

‘No,’ the rabbi admitted. ‘He had enemies too. And I will have to admit that if poor Cecil were alive, he would probably put me at the top of that list.’

‘You are surprising me, Rabbi.’

‘Ronnie.’

‘Sorry. Ronnie.’

‘Why am I surprising you?’

‘Well, you are a… in your position as a religious leader…’

‘My dear Chief Inspector Madison, I think you are confusing your religions somewhat. We, Jews, are not told to offer the other cheek. We are told, if someone aims to kill you, you get there first and kill him… or her,’ he added after a thought.

In the silence that followed, Rabbi Zimmerman realised what he’d just said and winced.

‘Sorry. That was in poor taste, considering the situation.’

‘Would this be your defence in the event of you being accused of this murder?’ Madison asked after a while.

‘You mean – was he out to kill me and I killed him first? I refuse to answer on the grounds of incriminating myself.’

Rabbi Zimmerman looked at Madison with an obvious glint in his eyes.

It was good to know that all the years he had put into studying law sometimes proved useful.

Madison smiled back. He could not help warming up to the old rabbi.

‘I will let you off the hook for now, Rab—Ronnie… I will

need a list of everyone who was at the synagogue this morning prior to your finding the body.'

'That's fine. I will get one of the secretaries to give you the list. No one gets in or out without their knowledge.'

'Thanks. Did Mr Kaufman have a family?'

'No children. Just a wife.'

'I need to go and tell his wife. Would you want to accompany me? Comfort her?'

'I don't think that would be a good idea,' the rabbi answered. 'I am the last person she would take comfort from.'

Chief Inspector Madison, although surprised, did not follow this with another question. Time enough to explore all that, but his investigative nose was beginning to itch.

4

PC Lisa Thompson was excited. Her sergeant had just informed her that Chief Inspector Madison requested her to join his team on a new investigation.

She had worked with Madison once before and could not wait to work with him again.

Her colleagues envied her being singled out like this, and therefore put out the theory that Madison fancied Lisa.

Secretly, Lisa wished that would be the case. She admired Madison. He was sharp, very clever, and did not suffer fools gladly. He was the rare combination of a strict boss that managed at the same time to be adored by the officers under his command. Lisa knew this new assignment would be hard work and she was looking forward to it.

Lisa had been a pretty little girl. The kind that people turned their heads in the street to have a better look at. She had blue eyes and long, wavy blonde hair. Lisa's mother had big plans for her beautiful daughter. She dressed her in pretty dresses and sent photos to many child agencies. Lisa even got to star in an ad that ran on television for a very short time. It was an ad for a children's clothing company that folded soon after airing the ad. Her mother assured Lisa that it had nothing to do with her ad.

As Lisa was growing up, she was sent for dancing lessons, drama lessons and even a course in make-up. Lisa enjoyed the dancing, but not the acting or make-up.

Growing up, she became more and more interested in her brother's activities – football, fighting, cycling, et cetera. The pretty dresses were hanging neglected in her cupboard and Lisa started borrowing clothes from her brother. T-shirts, trousers and the like.

It soon dawned on Mrs Thompson that her little girl was a tomboy and would never be a model or an actress. Lisa believed that to this day her mother had not grown out of her disappointment.

While watching films with her brother, Lisa became more and more fascinated by the women police officers – as tough and strong as the male officers – and early on made up her mind that this was the path she was going to follow. No amount of talking with her parents changed her mind. She was going to be a police officer and she would make a good one.

When her phone rang and she saw the identity of the caller clearly on the screen – Jack Madison – her heart missed a beat.

She answered her phone, trying to sound calm.

'Gov!' she said. 'Thank you for—'

She did not get any further.

'Lisa.' His deep voice came through on her phone. 'I will pick you up in half an hour. Will explain it all on the way.'

'Yes, gov,' she said, asking no questions. He said he would explain on the way. That was enough for her.

5

Half an hour gave Lisa just enough time to inform her sergeant that she was leaving, tidy her desk, run to the loo and even enough time to fix her make-up. At exactly twenty-nine minutes after the call, she was standing at the car park, where Madison could not miss her.

Madison was already there, waiting for her. He was still driving the metallic green Yeti and she hurried towards it.

'Am I late, gov?' she asked, knowing full well she was not.

'Get in, Lisa,' Madison said, holding the door open for her. 'You are not late and I'm glad Sergeant Madden agreed to release you.'

Lisa got in and closed the door after her.

'Sergeant Madden wouldn't dare say no to you, gov,' she said, smiling.

'Really?' Madison said, genuinely surprised. 'Useful information,' he added, smiling back.

Lisa wished Madison had not smiled at her. She had noticed before that his smile – powerful, arrogant and kind all at once – could render her speechless and immobile.

Keeping it short, Madison gave Lisa the main points of the day's events and explained why he wanted her to join him on this visit.

Lisa was thankful that her sergeant had reminded her to have a notebook and a pen with her.

'A tidy garden means a tidy person,' Madison remembered his training detective saying when impressing on his students the importance of observation. And indeed – there could be no doubt on first sight of the Kaufmans' abode. There was not a weed in sight. The plants were spaced at an exact and regular distance. The path between the beds was immaculately clean.

Cleaner than my kitchen floor, Lisa said to herself.

The house was freshly painted – a no nonsense white. Even the windows were shining in white, reflecting the sun and almost blinding the two officers.

DCI Madison and PC Lisa Thompson approached the house slowly. It was never a pleasant task, giving families bad news, and no matter how many times he had done it, Chief Inspector Madison never got used to it. He was also aware of the young PC accompanying him. It was Lisa's first time at this unpleasant task. He had asked her to accompany him because it was part of the job an officer had to tackle sooner or later.

'You OK?' he mumbled as they reached the door.

Before Lisa had the chance to reply, and before the inspector rang the doorbell, the door swung open.

'Well – you sure took your time!' The woman standing at the door was in her sixties, full figure but not very tall. She looked very angry.

Madison was somewhat thrown – not a state he regularly found himself in.

'Mrs Kaufman?' he managed to say.

'It takes ten minutes, at the most, driving from the synagogue to this house. I know, because I have done it plenty of times. So what took you so long?'

'Mrs Kaufman,' the chief inspector said, finding his more authoritative voice, 'I am DCI Madison and this is PC Lisa Thompson. Would it be OK if we came in?'

'I guess,' Mrs Kaufman said, and reluctantly moved sideways to let them in. 'Although I don't see the point. If you came to give me the news, you are too late. I have already had a few phone calls informing me of my husband's demise.'

They were standing in the small entrance hall and it did not look like Mrs Kaufman was going to invite them to sit down any time soon.

'I am really sorry, Mrs Kaufman,' the Chief Inspector started. 'We came as soon as we could.'

'It is not something you want to hear over the phone, DCI Madison!'

'I can only say again that I am very sorry. We asked the rabbi and the office staff not to tell you until we had—'

'But did you ask them not to tell anyone else?' Mrs Kaufman interrupted Madison. 'Because half the synagogue seems to have known about it before me. All the kind souls, who must be delighted at the news, saw fit to call me and say how sorry they were.'

Madison was lost for words, again a state rarely experienced by a policeman who thought he had seen it all. He hoped that Lisa Thompson did not get the impression that this was a common response from a bereaved relative.

'Mrs Kaufman, I am not sure how much people told you. Could we possibly sit down and talk?'

'You can come in here,' she said reluctantly, 'but I don't have a lot of time. There are things to arrange.'

She opened the first door leading from the hall. The two officers followed her into a small but very tidy, minimally furnished room. They eyed the three-piece suite, expecting to be invited to sit down, but no such invitation arrived.

Lisa always thought of small rooms as cosy and warm but this was small and freezing – and not just in temperature. Everything about the room was cold. The walls were white. No decoration or interesting features. There were no family photos or any pictures at all. A small television set sat in the corner of the room, facing the sofa. A couple of figurines stood on the mantelpiece. They seemed out of place in a room with so few ornaments.

'Is there anyone we can call for you?' Madison asked. 'A relative? Friend?'

'If I want to call anyone, DCI Madison, I will do so. I might be old but I can still work the phone!'

No one spoke for a while. Lisa took out her notebook and pen and tried to find a comfortable position to write, standing up.

'So? What happened to my husband?' Mrs Kaufman enquired, standing very upright and staring at Madison.

Mrs Kaufman was a really small woman, but standing upright as she did made her seem much taller than she was.

Madison was rarely made to feel so uncomfortable by a member of the public, particularly one just given the worst news.

'We don't yet have all the information regarding your husband's death, Mrs Kaufman,' he said. 'I'm sure you can appreciate – we have only just been made aware of it. All we know is that he seems to have fallen from the balcony in the synagogue.'

'The balcony? That's ridiculous,' Mrs Kaufman interrupted him. 'What was he doing up on the balcony? Only the choir ever goes up there.'

'We don't know yet, Mrs Kaufman. I was hoping maybe you could tell us.'

PC Thompson, with a surprising show of initiative, interrupted the two.

'Would you mind if I sit down, Mrs Kaufman?' she asked. 'It is very difficult to write standing up.'

Chief Inspector Madison was impressed. Most constables on their first 'outing' to a bereaved family member would be practically rigid with fear of saying or doing the wrong thing and would try to be invisible, and certainly inaudible.

Even Mrs Kaufman seemed to be taken aback at this audacity. She was lost for words and simply motioned the two to sit down.

'Thank you so much, Mrs Kaufman,' Lisa said, smiling her gratitude while taking a seat at the end of the sofa. She positioned her little pad on her knees and was ready to take notes.

Madison smiled to Lisa while his back was turned to Mrs Kaufman and sat down next to her.

Mrs Kaufman remained standing – just to make sure her guests were clear they were not welcome.

Madison was trying to regain the upper hand, feeling ridiculously small – he was just about six feet tall.

'Mrs Kaufman, did you see your husband this morning before he went to the synagogue?'

Mrs Kaufman looked down at Madison in contempt.

She spat her words out. 'Of course I did.'

'How did he seem to you?' Madison asked. 'Was he… any different than usual?'

'He was alive!' Mrs Kaufman replied. 'What else should I have noticed?'

Lisa jumped in, trying to ease the situation.

'Did he seem… worried or… stressed?'

For the first time, Mrs Kaufman seemed to have lost her composure. To Madison's relief, she sank into the armchair.

'Why… what do you mean?… Are you saying… that he would…?'

'At this stage,' Madison replied, 'we are trying to find out what happened.'

'You said that he fell from the balcony… what the hell he was doing up on that balcony only God knows. I have never known him go up there. Are you saying that he… that he did not fall… that he…?'

'I am not saying that,' Madison answered quickly. 'As of now, we don't know what happened.'

'You say that he never went up there,' Madison said after a short pause. 'Yet this morning he obviously did. We need to know why.'

'You think he went up there in order to jump? This is absurd! Cecil wouldn't… this is unthinkable.'

'Could he have been meeting someone on the balcony?'

'Meeting up in the balcony? Ridiculous. No one ever meets in the balcony. Unless… are you suggesting that someone lured him up there and then… pushed him?'

When he was back at home and writing notes about the case, Madison knew that he would surmise his questioning of the widow was flawed. At the same time, he wondered if there was any way of questioning this woman that wouldn't be flawed.

'Please don't distress yourself, Mrs Kaufman,' he said softly. 'Forgive my clumsy question.'

'I don't understand what you are trying to say.' Mrs Kaufman suddenly looked all of her five feet. Fragile and panicking – finally a human reaction to the dreadful news she had just heard.

'Can I get you a cup of tea, Mrs Kaufman?' Lisa interrupted the awkward moment.

She was smacked down before she managed to put down her writing pad and stand up.

'If I want a cup of tea, PC Thompson, in my own house, I will make it myself.'

'I'm so sorry. I didn't mean—'

'No one is allowed in my kitchen without my permission – and you certainly don't have it!'

'I was only trying to…' Lisa ran out of things to say.

Madison dived in to rescue her.

'We will leave you now, Mrs Kaufman. We are very sorry for your loss.' The chief inspector started getting up.

'The rabbi.'

'Sorry?' Madison thought that he had never encountered someone who could throw him off his composure like this woman seemed to do.

'You implied someone might have arranged to meet my husband up in the balcony in order to push him down. I'm saying it might have been the rabbi.'

'The rabbi? Surely… one doesn't think of a Rabbi in… these terms…'

'One doesn't think in these terms about a PROPER rabbi, Chief Inspector.'

After yet another awkward silence, Madison bravely tried again.

'Are you suggesting,' he asked, 'that the rabbi might have… harmed your husband?'

'This was your suggestion, Chief Inspector. I thought my husband fell to his death, but you suggested that someone might have hurt him.'

In the silence, Lisa sat back on the sofa and took out the notebook she had already disposed of in her handbag. She was getting ready for the questions that would follow Mrs Kaufman's extraordinary declaration.

'Why would the rabbi want to harm your husband, Mrs Kaufman?'

'Why? Because Cecil saw right through him. Because we exposed him to the board. That's why.'

'What exactly is it that your husband exposed, Mrs Kaufman?'

'That he is unfit to be a rabbi. He knew that sooner or later, we were going to expose him…'

Mrs Kaufman stood up determinedly.

'I don't want to talk to you any more,' she said. 'There are things I need to get on with.'

Madison stood up and Lisa followed him, quickly stuffing her notebook back into her bag.

'Well… thank you, Mrs Kaufman. We will leave you in peace now. If you are sure there is nothing we can do for you…'

The two officers could not get out of the house fast enough.

Safely outside, making sure he was out of earshot and eyeshot, Chief Inspector Madison mumbled, 'I'm beginning to think that Mr Kaufman threw himself off the balcony. Wouldn't you, in his place?'

Lisa Thompson hurried to the car, trying to choke the laughter she was losing control of. She suspected Mrs Kaufman was watching their every move from the window.

'It was so cold in there,' Lisa whispered, shivering. 'Is she doing her bit for global warming?'

'I have been in morgues that were cosier than that room,' he said, and unlocked the car.

6

THE TEAM

DCI Madison added two more people to the team that would be working on the synagogue case.

Sergeant Dave Brodmann and Madison had been friends for many years. They started in the police together as two fresh constables and became very close.

In time, their wives also became friends. Lily and Angi, Brodmann's wife, liked each other and often met for coffee or shopping. And the two couples got together for dinners at each other's houses.

After Lily died, Dave and Angi were there for Madison. At first, Dave stayed with Madison twenty-four-seven, afraid of what he might do.

With time, they all got into a new routine – Dave and Angi would invite Madison to come for a meal and he would, politely, turn them down. Being three together instead of the four they used to be was too painful.

Eventually Angi stopped inviting and Dave took Madison out to the pub as often as he could. Which became less and less often as Dave and Angi began to build their family. Dave became a father three times over and that seemed to be the most important thing in his life. He managed to make sergeant but never tried to go higher.

Madison, on the other hand, threw himself into his work and climbed the ladder with the speed of lightning. Those who did not relish his meteoric rise up the ranks comforted themselves by saying that his skin colour did the trick. The police needed to show they had some black high-ranking officers, they used to say. And Madison fitted the bill perfectly. He was well educated, well spoken, good-looking and very presentable. Perfect for public relations, tongues wagged.

Madison was aware of the whispering around his promotions but he did not allow it to touch him. The job was his life, and he kept putting his best into it.

Dave and Madison understood each other's needs and tendencies. There was no animosity or jealously between them. Just acceptance and deep affection for each other.

'A body in the synagogue?' Dave was astonished. 'A corpse in the attic?'

'No, Dave. Not a corpse. The body is freshly dead.'

Sergeant Brodmann agreed to join Madison's team.

7

Back at the synagogue, Chief Inspector Madison was seated in the rabbi's office, sipping a lukewarm cup of tasteless coffee. It was heaven.

'You look shattered, Chief Inspector,' Rabbi Zimmerman commented.

'Well – I just visited Mrs Kaufman,' the chief inspector replied.

The rabbi looked at the chief inspector for a while.

'I expect you need something stronger than our coffee. I keep a secret stash of whiskey for just such an occasion.' Rabbi Zimmerman stood up.

'Tempting, Rabbi – but I am on duty, so this coffee will have to do.'

As the rabbi was settling back in his chair, Madison said quietly, 'Not a fan, Mrs Kaufman. Is she?'

'I'm afraid not. Most definitely not a fan.'

'Amongst the people who might have wished to harm Mr Kaufman, you seem to be top of the list.'

'That bad?' the rabbi asked after a long silence. 'I knew she wasn't a fan but I didn't think it was that bad... I guess that puts me in an awkward position. I did discover the body.'

'Did you push Mr Kaufman off the balcony, Rabbi?'

'In my dreams – probably.' Rabbi Zimmerman smiled sadly. He noticed that the chief inspector was addressing him as Rabbi, in spite of his asking to be called Ronnie, but he let it go.

'Do you mind telling me what exactly happened between you and the Kaufmans to result in all this animosity?'

'It's a long story.'

'I like stories,' the chief inspector replied. 'The longer the better.'

'Well… it sounds bad talking about him now he's… well, I was here only a short time when he came to talk to me. He was already on the board but he wanted to be the chair. The chair has to be proposed by someone and then elected by the congregation. He thought that being proposed by the rabbi would give more weight to his standing… I told him I didn't want to interfere in anything remotely political. He didn't like it.'

The rabbi paused there.

Madison said nothing. He sensed there was more and gave the rabbi time.

'He was very subtle about it,' the rabbi continued. 'He would come in here, talking about this and that and then, very smoothly, let me know that he was aware of the reason I had to leave my post in the US and come to the UK.'

Again, Madison said nothing. He knew the rabbi was finding it difficult.

'You will learn about it sooner or later anyhow, so I'd better tell you myself,' the rabbi continued. 'I was one of the junior rabbis in a very big synagogue in New York. I was married at the time… not to Rachel, my present wife. Rachel was also married. We worked on a project together, teaching Hebrew through song. Rachel plays the piano and she has a lovely voice… We tried to stop it but it was stronger than us. Some people are lucky to meet the right person before they marry someone else. We were lucky to meet, but the timing was lousy. We broke up more times than I like to remember but it was no use... We knew from the start that we were meant to be together. It was a big scandal. We had to leave. Rachel has a daughter... She had to fight hard to keep her. She is living with us but goes back to New York often to see her father. When I interviewed for this job, I told the then-chair everything. He decided there was no need for everyone to know about it... fresh start and all that.'

'And Mr Kaufman knew about it? How?'

'I have been asking myself that ever since. I have no idea. But he did know.'

'In other words, he was blackmailing you?'

'He tried to, yes. But I knew that if I gave in to him once, it would never stop. In a meeting of the board, I told them everything. I didn't tell them about Cecil... Mr Kaufman. He was at that meeting. Sat there saying nothing. I offered my resignation but they were having none of it. By that time, I'd gained some popularity with the congregation, and in any case... everyone was delighted to have a "normal" rabbi married to a woman... The former one was gay. I think the congregation felt they had done their bit for political correctness and could appoint a straight man again without feeling guilty about it...'

Madison had come across blackmail many times in the past but he never expected to find it in a place of worship.

'Rabbi,' he asked after a while, 'if Mr Kaufman tried to blackmail you – the rabbi, no less – is there a chance he was blackmailing anyone else? That would certainly provide us with a motive.'

Rabbi Zimmerman paused for a minute.

'I have wondered the same thing myself, Chief Inspector,' he admitted finally, 'but I have heard nothing to that effect.'

The rabbi was lost in thought.

'Chief Inspector,' he said after a while, 'is it not too early to be looking for suspects? After all, we don't even know yet that it wasn't an accident… or a suicide. He could have tripped and lost his balance and—'

'Sorry, Rabbi,' Madison interrupted him. 'I'm afraid Mr Kaufman was definitely pushed. He was hit on the side of the head before being pushed down… so there is no doubt. We are talking murder here.'

8

DAY 2

DCI Madison and his team had worked in some strange places, but this was the first time they had convened in a car.

'Sorry about this,' Madison said, sitting quite comfortably in the driver's seat – plenty of leg room – of his old, metallic green Yeti. PC Lisa Thompson and PC Benson sat in the back seat, their knees knocking against the front seats, while Sergeant Brodmann, being older and rather larger, had settled down in the roomy front passenger seat.

Josh Benson had been an awkward child. It was as if he never felt comfortable being a child, or rather, being much cleverer than the other children. He did not excel in any sport. In fact, he always did his best to avoid the sport lessons. He always felt that being sporty, tall and handsome was so much more desirable than being clever. Academically, everything came easy. He never appreciated this gift he was given, of being able to understand maths, chemistry, physics. He would gladly have given all that up to be a football star.

But that was not what fate had designed for him. He went to university and chose science and computer sciences.

In his final year, an officer from the police force came to talk to the students. He worked hard to convince them their expertise in the sciences would be very useful for the police and would be well rewarded.

Suddenly, Benson saw a way to combine his mental ability with a job that could become physical. He started spending time at the local gym, working on his fitness. He built up stamina, running on the treadmill, lifting weights and more. He started developing muscles that, in spite of his science degree, he did not know he possessed.

By the time he graduated, Benson was able to pass the physical tests and join the police.

When Madison took up the investigation of the body in the synagogue, he asked Dave Brodmann if he knew of a young PC who would prove useful as a member of the team. Madison liked to choose young police officers and help train them in the business.

Dave Brodmann had already noticed PC Benson. In spite of trying to blend in, Benson was clearly an odd one out. He was obviously extremely bright – well above the other recruits – and he was so keen to learn the job that Brodmann had no problem recommending him to Madison.

Josh Benson could not believe his luck. Although new, he had heard the name Chief Inspector Madison mentioned many times. Everyone wanted to work with Madison. Madison always got the pick of the cases and had a record in solving his cases. And here he was, a new recruit, on his first mission – and working with Chief Inspector Madison.

Josh Benson was beyond excited.

Sitting in the back seat of Madison's green Yeti, he was secretly pinching himself, hoping that PC Thompson did not notice.

Madison gave his team a short summary of the case so

far. Thompson and Benson were taking notes in the back seat. Brodmann was listening attentively.

'From tomorrow morning we can use the caretaker's room as our incident room,' Madison informed his team. 'It will be a little more roomy than this car, but not much. It will have to do. Benson – you will have to prepare the room. A list and photos of everyone who was present at one time or another in the synagogue on Thursday. We have to treat everyone who was there as a suspect. So, as much detail as you can get about them all. I hear you are something of a wizard with computers?'

Josh could feel his cheeks flushing. He wished Lisa – PC Thompson – was not watching him quite so intently.

'I can do computers, yes, gov,' he said.

'Well, I want you to collate all the information the team gathers and put it together in a way that will be accessible to all of us mortals. The department will provide us with a computer and everything that you need to work it. Would that be OK?'

'Yes, gov,' Josh said.

'Good. Lisa, I want you to have a talk with the secretary. In my experience, secretaries know a lot – probably more than they care to reveal. See what you can get out of her. Brodmann, you can take the day off tomorrow because you will be working on Saturday.'

'Jack?'

'You will accompany me to the service at the synagogue, Brodmann. I understand it starts at ten thirty and lasts about two hours. I have never been to a synagogue service, so I will need you to guide me.'

'I'm sorry, Jack. I have never been to a service in, er… this kind of synagogue.'

'This kind? What kind is this?'

'Reform. I am more… kind of… Orthodox.'

'Are you, Sergeant Brodmann?' Madison faked amazement. 'Did I not see you plenty of times tucking into a bacon sandwich?'

'I am not Orthodox. I just… I belong to the Orthodox synagogue. I have never belonged to any other synagogue. I would be completely lost in a reform one.'

'How different can it be?' Madison enquired. 'They are Jewish… You are Jewish. You'll be fine.'

Brodmann looked very unhappy.

'It is the wife's birthday on Saturday,' Brodmann muttered. 'I was going to take her out.'

'Well, why don't you bring her with? That would count as taking her out, wouldn't it?'

9

DAY 3

PC Benson was very proud of his handiwork. The little room that used to be the caretaker's hidey-hole had had a real makeover. Gone were the vacuum cleaners, the brooms, the brushes, the many cleaning fluids. In fact, only one thing remained – the kettle, but one would hardly recognise it, as it had been polished within an inch of its life. There were eight pristine cups on the shelf – PC Benson brought those from his mother's house. He intended each member of the team to have two cups to drink from before needing to do any washing up.

In the corner of the room, on a little desk, proudly stood a state-of-the-art computer and next to it pens, papers and the like. Overhead Benson had hung the enormous screen which he had picked up from head office early that morning. The screen was touch sensitive and came with a pointing stick that worked the screen in place of a finger.

All signs of the room's previous use had been removed, which meant the room seemed quite a bit bigger. The window was open wide, allowing fresh air to pour in. With any luck it would soon get rid of the overpowering disinfectant smell.

Mrs Benson had given her son a white tablecloth that was now proudly covering the little table in the other corner of the room. A biscuit tin was sitting in the middle of the table. Mrs Benson's cream cheese cookies would soon become a firm favourite with the team.

The smell of freshly brewed tea welcomed Chief Inspector Madison and PC Thompson as they entered the incident room.

'Well, Benson,' Madison proclaimed, eyeing the little room, 'what a transformation. Have you been at it all night?'

'Almost' would have been the correct answer. Benson had had a word with Mr Jonson, the caretaker and, being the police, Jonson let him have a set of the synagogue's keys and the code for the alarm.

Armed with those, Benson arrived at the synagogue at seven in the morning, which gave him enough time to work on the room and arrange it into the office the team would be using during this investigation.

'Not quite all night, gov,' Benson replied. 'The synagogue is not open at night. I thought… just wanted to make the place a little more pleasant to work in.'

'You have done us proud, Benson. Thank you.'

'Would you like a cup of tea and a biscuit, gov?'

'I could get used to this.' Madison smiled at Benson and winked cheekily at Lisa. 'That would be lovely, thank you.'

Lisa smiled back and tried to ignore the fact that her heart missed a beat.

PC Benson got busy with pouring two cups of tea and serving it with a couple of cookies each on the side.

Lisa Thompson took a bite of the cookie and could not believe the flavours that exploded on her palate.

'OMG!' she exclaimed. 'This is utterly scrumptious. You didn't make these, did you?'

'Afraid not,' Benson admitted sheepishly. 'These are kind of my mother's pièce de résistance.'

Madison took a bite of the cookie and agreed with Lisa.

'Really delicious,' he said. 'Can we look forwards to a daily supply?'

'I'll see what I can do, gov.'

'Before we continue – while in this room, there is no need for titles and ranks. I will address you as Lisa and Josh and you can address me as Jack. Sergeant Brodmann – when he is here – will be addressed as Dave. Saves a lot of time.'

'Yes, gov,' Benson said. 'I mean – Jack.'

No one had ever made her name sound so alluring, Lisa thought. Madison's voice was deep and resonant. She had heard people using the word 'velvet' to describe fine voices. She now knew what they meant, only she would probably add 'chocolate' to the description. When Madison spoke, it was more like singing, and the sound of her name pronounced by him reverberated deep in her body.

'So, Josh, let's go through the list of suspects.'

Josh Benson was in his element. Here he was, involved in a big investigation, allowed to do what he loved most – working computer magic to help catch a killer.

'List of suspects coming up,' Josh said. He brought up the list of suspects on the big screen. He used the clever stick to point at each name as he mentioned them.

'So, this is a list of everyone who was at the synagogue on the morning of the murder up to twelve twenty-five, which is when the body was discovered. Top of the list – the rabbi. According to himself – and the secretaries confirm – until he walked into the synagogue and found the body, he had been in his room.

'Then – the caretaker, Jon Jonson. Apparently, he was working outside in the car park most of the day. Building a shed or something – for storage. He came in long before Mr Kaufman, said 'hi' to the secretaries, picked up his tools and went out. The secretaries did not see him come back in but, working at the side of the building, he could have come in and out without being seen. He has all the keys to the synagogue.'

Jack and Lisa were taking notes while listening to Josh going through the list on the board.

'Then we have the two secretaries,' Josh continued. 'The senior one – Jane Barker. Lisa talked to her, so she can fill us in on that conversation in a minute. The other one – Becky Mosco. Quite a bit older than Miss Barker. Straightforward, as far as I can tell. Quite happy to talk to us.

'Next one is Miki Solomon. Interesting. She was the music director until recently when she resigned. No one wants to talk about it much, but I gather she had a big do with the victim and the result was that she resigned. Not a bad motive…'

Madison looked up from his notes.

'Hmmm,' he muttered. 'Almost too obvious. What was she doing at the synagogue if she had resigned?'

'Apparently, she came in to collect some music she'd left behind. Interestingly, she not only had to go into the synagogue for the music, but she would have had to go up to the balcony. Apparently, that was where the choir rehearsed, and she kept her music in the storage cupboard up there.'

'Did she indeed?' Madison chewed on the end of his pen. 'Like I said – it would be too easy and obvious, wouldn't it? But let's not dismiss a suspect simply because they are too perfect for the part.'

After a short silence, Madison turned to Lisa.

'So, Lisa, you had a talk with Jane Barker. How did that go?'

'Not sure, gov—Jack. She is a nervous person. The whole thing is very unsettling for her, whereas the other secretary –

Becky – seemed to be dealing with it so much more calmly. To be fair, the office was extremely busy – nonstop phone calls and emails and people coming in. But it almost seemed like Jane welcomed the interruptions because she really didn't want to talk to me. If we can get her away from the office at some stage, it might be easier to talk to her.'

'Well done, you two,' Madison said while helping himself to another cookie. 'One for the road,' he added and stood up. 'We made a start. Have a good weekend. Will see you all here Monday morning.'

10

DAY 4

At the Kaufmans' home, things were reaching boiling point.

Mrs Kaufman was taking off one coat and trying on another one. Sheila, her sister, stood by the door, car keys in her hand at the ready.

'I think this one is good, Linda,' Sheila said, trying to hide her exasperation.

'I don't know,' muttered Mrs Kaufman. 'It's too… pretty. I can imagine what the kind hearts would say about that… rigor mortis has barely settled and here she is looking all pretty…'

No one would accuse you of looking pretty, Sheila said to herself.

'Linda,' she said aloud, 'if that's what they will say, I don't know why you bother to go at all. Why are you putting yourself through it?'

'I'll take this one – the black one. It's smart but not in your face.'

Mrs Kaufman finally put the black coat on and walked to the door.

'You don't have to go, Linda.'

'Yes, I do. You don't understand. I want to look them all in the eye and make them feel guilty. One way or the other – they all killed him.'

Mrs Kaufman marched down the drive and got into the car on the driver's side.

'Keys,' she snapped at her sister, holding her hand for the keys.

'Are you sure you are up to driving?' Sheila asked.

'Quite sure. I will show them they don't break me this easily.'

Mrs Kaufman started the car and as she pressed the accelerator the car jumped forwards and Sheila barely had the time to close the passenger door.

'Linda!' she shouted. 'My leg was still out!'

'Sorry,' Mrs Kaufman muttered under her breath. She did not sound all that sorry.

Sheila buckled up and said nothing while Mrs Kaufman started up the road towards the synagogue.

'I don't understand you, Linda,' Sheila said after a while. 'You hate these people so much yet you two seem to have spent most of your life with them.'

'In case you hadn't noticed, Sheila, one of "us two" is no longer able to spend any time with anyone!'

'You know what I mean. You both worked so hard to get Cecil on the board, and even harder to get him voted chair. Only for him to be voted out in no time. Why do you want to keep going there?'

Mrs Kaufman didn't immediately reply. She put her foot down and drove too fast, but Sheila said nothing.

'I know what you are trying to say, Sheila. You never liked Cecil. Did you?'

'Really, Linda. Why bring that up now?'

'We are here. Enough talking.'

Mrs Kaufman parked the car in the synagogue's car park and got out of the car, ready to face the people she had just accused of killing her husband.

11

Madison parked outside Brodmann's house and turned off the engine. He expected Brodmann to wait till the last possible moment to come out.

To his delight, the door opened and it was Angi who came out of the house, wearing a dress and an impressive hat on her head.

Madison walked out of his car and greeted her with a fond hug.

'Well,' he said, 'this is a pleasant surprise.'

'Surprise?' Angi was very fond of Madison and faked her amazement. 'I thought you told Dave he could bring me?'

'I absolutely did,' Madison concurred, 'but I really didn't think you would like to come. Happy birthday, Angi. What is it – thirty-six?'

Angi slapped him fondly on his arm.

'Don't be facetious, Jack,' she said. 'Actually, I have been curious about this synagogue for a while. But I wouldn't quite call it a birthday treat.'

Madison opened the passenger door and helped Angi get in.

'So, do you have any plans for after the service? I would like to treat you two to a nice meal. As an apology.'

'That would be nice, Jack. We had plans, but they had to be cancelled, so I will accept on behalf of both of us.'

Madison got into the driver's seat and looked at his watch.

'I really don't want to be late,' he said. 'Maybe we should go without Dave? I'm sure you could instruct me just as well – better – on what is going on at the synagogue?'

'Yes, maybe we should,' Angi said, just as Dave came out of the house, locking the door behind him.

'Hurry up, Dave!' Angi called out.

'I'm coming,' Dave muttered and walked to the car. He got in the back seat and put his belt on.

'Jack is taking us for a slap-up meal after the service,' Angi said as Madison started the car.

'Is he?' Brodmann made it clear he was not impressed.

'Oh, cheer up, for goodness' sake, Dave. You would think Jack was daring you to a bungee jump.'

They drove in silence for a while.

Jack broke the silence. 'Don't we have to wear something on our heads?'

'This is a reform synagogue!' Dave answered.

'So – they don't cover their heads at the reform synagogue?'

'Honestly, Jack – I don't know what they do and don't do at this synagogue,' Dave replied. 'Like I said – I belong to the Orthodox one.'

'I am convinced the rabbi was wearing one… a… what's it called?'

'A yarmulke,' Dave offered, grudgingly.

'Right. Shouldn't we be wearing one?'

'I wouldn't have thought they bother about it here,' Dave said. He glanced at his watch. He'd rather have been anywhere but where he was going.

'You didn't bring a… yamulthingie with you? I was hoping you would have a spare one for me.'

'Sorry. I didn't.'

'How many of these things do you have at home?'

'How many… yarmulkes?'

'Yeah… yarmulkes… Two? Three?'

'About…'

'Or more? Five? Six?'

'Not that many.'

Brodmann kept glancing at his wife, seated next to Madison. He fully expected her to barge in and scold him, but she was silent.

'You knew you were going to a synagogue and you didn't think—'

'I don't call this a synagogue.'

'Seriously? You have a big problem, man. Big problem.'

'If they want you to wear a yarmulke, they will have some spare ones by the door.'

'There you go, Dave. That's what I needed you here for. Yarmulkes by the door. Excellent.'

12

They arrived at the synagogue with five minutes to spare.

'Here,' Angi said, producing two yarmulkes out of her bag. 'Wear these.'

'You are a star, Angi,' Madison said, and put his yarmulke on.

Dave could not believe this.

'You let us go on about it and never said you had these two all along,' he said, clearly annoyed.

Angi smiled triumphantly.

'I enjoyed watching you squirm,' she said, and gave him the second yarmulke, while glancing at Madison, who was clearly enjoying this little scene.

Angi watched Madison putting on the yarmulke and could not help laughing.

'You look ridiculous, Jack,' she said, trying to adjust the yarmulke on his head.

'Is that a racist remark?' Madison asked provocatively.

'Probably,' Angi said, wiping tears of laughter away. 'I have never seen a black man wearing a yarmulke.'

'Definitely racist,' Madison said and bent down to look at himself in the driver's mirror. 'I think it suits me,' he declared, straightening and locking the car.

Dave put his yarmulke on, making it obvious he was doing so under duress.

The three walked into the foyer. Rabbi Zimmerman, who was welcoming people at the door, spotted them and walked over.

'Nice to see you here, Chief Inspector,' he said in a soft voice. 'Thanks for not coming in uniform,' he added.

'This is Sergeant Dave Brodmann,' Madison introduced him, 'and his dear wife, Angi Brodmann.'

The rabbi shook Dave and Angi's hands.

'Pleasure to meet you both,' he said. 'Is this your first time here?'

It was obvious to Madison that the rabbi spotted their Jewishness.

Brodmann was about to answer, but Angi got in first.

'It is,' she said. 'I'm really looking forward to it.'

'I hope you won't be disappointed,' the rabbi said, and handed them three prayer books. 'There will be a lot of Hebrew in the service,' he explained, 'but if you follow the siddur, you will see that everything is translated.'

'Siddur is the prayer book,' Angi said, softly.

As they were settling into their seats, Madison noticed Mrs Kaufman walking into the synagogue. She was dressed in black and was accompanied by another woman. The two walked towards the front row.

Madison followed with interest the steady trickle of people who quietly came to speak to Mrs Kaufman and shake her hand. He assumed they were uttering words of comfort, but not one of them stayed to talk. There were no signs of intimacy of any kind – no one bent over low enough to give Mrs Kaufman a hug. It seemed like they all said as little as possible before moving on and allowing another person to pay their respect. The relief on their faces as they moved away was palpable.

As if reading his mind, Angi Brodmann leant over to him.

'Well, this is kind of cold,' she whispered.

'Is that unusual?' Madison whispered back.

'I'd say. I have never seen a bereaved person greeted so coldly.'

At that moment, Rabbi Zimmerman walked into the synagogue hall. Not betraying any awkwardness, he walked over to Mrs Kaufman and offered his hand – a gesture that was ignored by her. He clearly muttered a few words and moved on to take his place in front of the congregation.

'This is going to be interesting,' Angi whispered in Madison's ear.

Madison thought how lucky it was that Dave took his remark seriously and brought Angi along. She was going to be a lot more useful than Dave.

Madison turned to his sergeant, who was sitting on his other side, to seek his reaction to this public display of contempt, and found him sitting on the edge of his chair, as if in physical pain.

'Are you OK?' Madison asked as quietly as his booming voice allowed him.

'What? I'm fine… Why?'

'Well, for goodness' sake, man – sit back on the chair,' Madison scolded Brodmann under his breath. 'I don't want you falling out of the chair and creating a scene.'

The rabbi was being extra helpful, providing page numbers and a little explanation here and there. The congregation sang a few hymns – nothing like the hymns sung at church, on the odd occasions that Madison attended one.

In quite a few of the hymns he noticed that Angi joined the singing in full voice. She'd always had a good voice.

He looked over at Brodmann. He was definitely not singing. The look on his face became more painful by the minute.

'Do you not know this tune?' Madison whispered. 'Angi seems to know it.'

Brodmann threw a glance at his wife and raised his eyebrows in frustration.

Madison returned to the prayer book and followed the English text with the help of the rabbi's occasional illuminating remarks.

People from the congregation came up in turn and read from the Bible. Everyone was reading in Hebrew.

Angi leant towards him and whispered, 'Every week a section of the Bible is read in Hebrew. It is an honour to be invited to read.'

Madison found it very interesting. Although he had no knowledge of Hebrew at all, he was fascinated with the different accents the Hebrew was read in. Some were more fluent than others and some clearly found reading in Hebrew very difficult.

The rabbi addressed the congregation and announced the reading of the Kaddish. He invited Mrs Kaufman to come on the bimah, but she declined.

'I will say it from here,' she said.

Angi whispered in Madison's ear, 'This is the prayer for the dead. Traditionally said by a relative of the dead person.'

Mrs Kaufman stood up and the rest of the congregation stood with her as she read the prayer, fluently and loudly, not bothering to look at the prayer book her sister was holding up for her.

She finished reading and the congregation replied with a loud 'Amen'.

Then, to everyone's surprise, Mrs Kaufman picked up her bag and, without saying a word, walked out of the synagogue.

Her companion was as surprised as everyone else. She hurriedly collected her handbag and the prayer book and rushed out after Mrs Kaufman.

In the silence that followed, the rabbi started the congregation in a song which gained in volume as it went along.

Once the rabbi was confident the congregation was more relaxed, he walked down from the bimah and stopped by Madison.

'Chief Inspector,' he said softly. 'I wonder – would you agree to talk to the congregation? Everyone is a little on edge.'

Madison was taken aback. He'd come to observe, not to give speeches.

'Rabbi – I don't have much to say. I am as much in the dark as your congregation.'

'I know, but if you wouldn't mind just taking a few questions, to reassure people.'

Madison stood up. How on earth was he going to reassure people about a murder that happened only three days earlier and presented no obvious clues or motives?

Madison glanced at his sergeant, hoping for some offer of help, but Brodmann was busy looking at his shoes and trying to hide a gleeful smile.

Madison followed the rabbi onto the bimah. The rabbi pointed him to the microphone, but Madison declined. He knew his voice could carry to far greater distances than the little synagogue hall.

Rabbi Zimmerman addressed the elephant in the room.

'I would like to introduce Detective Chief Inspector Jack Madison,' he started. 'Chief Inspector Madison is in charge of the investigation of… the terrible thing that happened here last Wednesday. He has kindly agreed to answer a few of your questions, so if there is anything you want to ask the chief inspector, could you please put your hand up and I will try to spot you.'

As usually happened in Q&A sessions, people were hesitating to ask the first question, but once someone was brave enough to ask, many more hands went up.

'I am sure you will all appreciate,' Madison started, 'that

the investigation is in its very early stages, and so, there is not much I can tell you at present. I will answer a few questions to the best of my ability, which, right now, is limited.'

Rabbi Zimmerman invited the owner of the first hand to come up to speak.

'Chief Inspector,' the man said, as Madison noted to himself that, even in a Jewish place of worship, where Jewish women reportedly were strong, it was the men who put their hands up first. 'The fact that there is an investigation means that it is definite that what happened was not an accident?'

Madison took a minute to reply.

'This is very early on in this case, so nothing definite yet, but yes, it looks like it was not an accident.'

There were now many hands up.

The rabbi picked one of the women.

'Are you assuming that it was… well, that someone… I mean – maybe he jumped? He was very unhappy because he was voted off the board… Maybe he… We can't assume that someone…'

Madison knew, of course, that before falling, Mr Kaufman was attacked, but he was not going to reveal this to the assembled congregation.

'You are quite right, madam,' Madison replied. 'And we are not assuming anything. At this stage anything is possible.'

The next person to ask a question did not wait for the rabbi to point to him.

'But you clearly think he was pushed,' the gentleman said, accusingly. 'In which case, we are all your suspects. Right?'

Madison knew this Q&A session was not a good idea and it was proving so.

The rabbi intervened.

'It is very good of the chief inspector to agree to answer your questions, but please remember he is here to help.'

One woman stood up and spoke in a soft voice.

'Chief Inspector – it is just that we are worried… scared even. This place has been home for us for many years. Nothing like this has ever happened.'

'I understand,' Madison said reassuringly. 'And we will do our best to clear this matter up as soon as possible, so that you can all again feel safe in this place. And let me finish by saying that we have taken over Mr Jonson's room and so, during hours that the synagogue is open, there will be at least one of our team present at the synagogue. If you have any worries or if there is anything you remember or think might be useful – the slightest thing – please knock on the door and come in and tell us. Don't think that anything you might remember is too trivial. Sometimes it's the most trivial things that solve a case.'

The rabbi took a clue from Madison declaring the session was finishing.

'Chief Inspector – in the name of everyone here – I would like to thank you for speaking to us and for working hard to bring this matter to a close.'

There was a murmur of agreement and people started making their way out of the synagogue.

Later, while driving to the restaurant, Madison laid into Brodmann.

'What was that all about, Dave?' he said, finally using his voice to its maximum volume. 'Sitting on the edge of the seat, trying not to make contact. I'm surprised you didn't have your feet dangling up in the air.'

'Leave it, Jack,' Brodmann snapped. 'Just leave it.'

But Madison was not about to.

'Is that how you behave when you go to church?' Madison asked.

'I don't go to church!' Brodmann snapped.

'What? You have never been to a church?'

'Of course I have been to a church,' Brodmann said, trying to control his anger.

'So – I'm asking – is that how you sit in a church?'

'No, it's not!'

'So, you are quite happy for your ass to fill a chair in a church, but not in a reform synagogue?'

'It's different!'

'Yes, it is different. Here you were with other Jews, at a Sabbath service where I could see you were following it perfectly well – turning the pages at the right time and following the Hebrew text. You should have been feeling at home!'

'You don't understand.'

'No, I don't understand. Please enlighten me.'

In the silence that followed, Madison was negotiating the heavy traffic of Saturday midday while Brodmann was trying to find the words to explain his reluctance.

'It's precisely the fact that they are using almost the same service,' Brodmann ventured, 'that annoys us… me. They are conducting it in a way which goes against all the laws and meanings of the traditional service. They are prostituting the traditional service… I haven't got the words to really explain it.'

'Dave,' Madison said after a while. 'We have been friends for more years than I care to remember. We worked together, we partied together, we got drunk in the pub together – and in all that time, I don't remember you ever talking about your religion… your Judaism… the synagogue. I never would have thought any of it was so important to you.'

'It's not,' Brodmann conceded. 'We could've gone ten more years without talking about it if you hadn't forced me to come to this synagogue with you.'

Angi, who had been watching the men arguing with a little sly smile in the corner of her mouth, finally spoke.

'Well, I found the service fascinating,' she declared. 'I think I will come again.'

'If you do,' Brodmann snapped, 'you will be doing it without me.'

'Good. I would enjoy it so much more without you.'

Madison was curious.

'Why?' he asked. 'What did you like about the service?'

'I liked hearing women reading from the Torah. That's the Bible. Why shouldn't women be reading from the Torah? Honestly, we are still doing it the way they did hundreds of years ago. Men doing all the important things and women doing the kiddush.'

'Kiddush?' Madison asked.

'That's what we did at the end. The rabbi saying blessing over food and drink and everyone tucks in. The women do the food and the service and the cleaning afterwards, while the men do the reading and the praying. In what other situation these days would women put up with this? They would be screaming discrimination – probably take you to court. Yet in synagogue, they all accept it.'

Madison parked his car and, as the three walked towards the entrance to the restaurant, Dave said, 'Are we going to change the subject or are we going to talk about synagogues the whole afternoon? I already have indigestion.'

'Must be all those fried fish balls you tucked into at the kiddush,' Angi said. 'You know fried food doesn't agree with you.'

Madison wanted to point out that eating the food at the synagogue was 'kosher' and sitting on the chairs was not, but he really wanted them to enjoy the meal, so decided against it.

A waiter approached their table with the menus.

'What is the most expensive item on your menu?' Brodmann asked. 'I'll have that.'

'Dave!' Angi protested. 'Behave yourself.'

'I'll have the same,' Madison told the waiter with an amused smile.

Angi ordered salad and, as the waiter walked off, a moment of silence descended on the table.

Angi was the first to break the silence.

'What's up with the merry widow?' she asked. 'She was so rude. First not coming up when the rabbi invited her, and then walking out at the end of the Kaddish. I have never seen anyone behave like that.'

'Well, she thinks the rabbi killed her husband.' Dave threw the remark and immediately caught Madison's look of disapproval.

Madison never allowed friendship to get in the way of their work, and Dave had just let drop a bit of information that Madison told him on the job.

Angi knew the two of them well and could tell Dave had overstepped the mark.

She looked from the one to the other and then turned to Madison.

'Well, Jack,' she started. 'Did you manage to follow the service or was it all a bit strange?'

Madison did not answer immediately. He was still staring at Brodmann, who was doing his best to avoid Madison's eyes.

Then, in an obvious decision to let the matter drop, Madison turned to look at Angi.

'I think I got quite a lot of it,' he answered. 'I was surprised by the cold, not to say hostile, atmosphere. I expected to see people hugging Mrs Kaufman... showing some sympathy... warm feelings. Isn't that the sort of thing you people do?'

'Us people?'

'You know what I mean, Dave. You are supposed to be so much warmer and more loving than we are. I saw no sign of that towards Mrs Kaufman. Mind you, from the little I have seen of her, I don't suppose she would have welcomed it…'

Angi was grateful that Madison dropped the 'attitude'. It could have been very unpleasant. She could sense that Dave was also relieved.

'Who is being a racist now?' she threw at Madison with a little superior smile.

All was well again and the three enjoyed the rest of their afternoon together.

13

DAY 6 (DAY 5 WAS A SUNDAY)

Monday morning started with a short get-together of Madison's team in the incident room. It might have been the smallest incident room Madison had worked in, but it was more welcoming than most.

PC Benson quickly memorised how each member of the team liked their coffee or tea, and he was offering them around while Madison was trying to give out tasks for the day.

'PC Benson,' Madison started in his official voice. 'This is not a tearoom. This is an incident room. Please don't spoil this lot too much. Next, they will be expecting cupcakes with their cups of tea.'

'Yes, sir… No, sir. No cupcakes.'

'Right,' Madison said, enjoying sipping a cup of tea perfectly made to his liking. 'So – Dave – I would like you to visit Mrs Kaufman.'

Brodmann almost choked on his perfect black coffee.

Madison smiled.

'Get off your high horse, Dave,' he said. 'You are the obvious person to go talk to her. She might warm to you where she can't to the rest of us. I want you to find out why she, and presumably her husband, have so few friends in the congregation. You never know – you might even find a little bit of a motive there.'

'First I am forced to spend Saturday – my wife's birthday – at the Reform's Shabbat service – three hours I will never get back – and now this.'

'I hear from the rabbi that Mrs Kaufman makes delicious lemon drizzle cake. Apparently, she used to bribe members of the board with it to help her husband be elected chair. If you play your cards right, you might get to sample it.'

Brodmann put down his coffee with a semi-violent movement that made Lisa jump. He then left the room in a huff.

'What do you want me to do, gov—Jack?' Lisa asked. 'I'm ready for anything, now the worst job is already taken.'

Madison emptied his cup of tea and got up.

'I want you to talk to the second secretary – Becky Mosco? See what gossip you can get out of her – hopefully she is more forthcoming than Miss Barker. I will meet with the rabbi, and after that will have a go at Miss Barker. Benson – sorry, I forgot your name?'

'Josh, er… Jack.' Benson was drying his hands after washing all the cups and putting them back in the cupboard.

'Right, Josh… when you are done with the housework, I would like you to talk to the caretaker. I want to know exactly where he was throughout the morning and what he saw or heard. People tend to walk past caretakers as if they are part of the furniture and often are not too guarded at what they say in their earshot. Maybe he heard things. We will meet here again at five this afternoon and exchange information.'

14

'Do come in,' Rabbi Zimmerman said when Madison knocked at his door. He motioned at the empty chair next to him and the chief inspector sat down. Madison had to admit to himself that he liked the rabbi – professionally not advisable. Madison couldn't quite put his finger on what he liked about the man but, coming as they did from such different backgrounds, he wondered at the ease with which he found himself relating to the rabbi.

'I glanced at your "incident room", Chief Inspector. Very impressive. I assume you have had a superior cup of coffee and therefore will not insult your palate by offering you our brand.'

Madison smiled.

'That's very understanding of you, Rabbi,' he said.

'Understanding is one of the requisites of my job.'

'Mine too, as it happens, Rabbi.'

Rabbi Zimmerman studied Madison's face for a little while, a knowing smile barely visible on his own face.

'I guess you had some problem understanding the service on Saturday?'

'That too, but I had my sergeant and his wife with me explaining it all.'

'Your sergeant is Jewish, then?'

'Only on Yom Kippur, I understand. Does that disqualify him?'

The rabbi laughed.

'Not at all. You are born Jewish. You don't really have a choice in the matter, and if he goes to synagogue on Yom Kippur, he is doing better than many.'

'He was... uncomfortable at the service. The little bit of observing he does, he does in the Orthodox synagogue.'

'Oh, yes. I understand. It's a funny thing... for the antisemites we are all equally Jewish. But to other Jews we are not Jewish at all.'

'I thought my sergeant was peculiar in that regard, but you say this is a common sentiment amongst Orthodox Jews?'

'Indeed. Are you surprised to find intolerance amongst the Jewish community? Our treatment by the Nazis did not make us better people than most people – although much of the world thinks it should have.'

Madison pondered this for a while.

'I was quite taken with the atmosphere in the synagogue on Saturday.' Madison returned to the business at hand. After all, he was here to investigate a murder, not to have a philosophical tête-à-tête with the rabbi.

'Well, Chief Inspector... a dead body was discovered in the synagogue, right by the holy Torah books. That would explain the difficult atmosphere last Shabbat.'

'Forgive me, Rabbi... that was insensitive. But actually I was referring to Mrs Kaufman's interaction with the congregation – or lack of it.'

'Ah... you noticed.'

'It was hard not to. I expected people to be sympathetic... concerned. There was none of that. Some came to shake her hand – doing their duty, it seemed – but most preferred to ignore her. Can you explain?'

The rabbi was obviously not comfortable with this subject.

'You met her, Chief Inspector. You can draw your own conclusions.'

'Many people resent the police on these occasions. You never know how a bereaved relative will react when you give them the dreadful news. Some actually blame us – as if we should be able to prevent any and all murders. But I didn't expect her to have alienated the whole congregation.'

'It is very sad, particularly now when Mrs Kaufman could do with some support. The lady who came with her was her sister but I didn't notice much affection between the two. The Kaufmans joined the synagogue a short time before I came. They are relatively new in the area. From what I knew, Mrs Kaufman wanted to join the local Orthodox synagogue, but Cecil – Mr Kaufman – was keen on coming here.'

'I sent my sergeant to visit with her this morning. I thought maybe they would have something in common. I hope she doesn't eat him alive.'

15

Sergeant Brodmann sat in his car for a while, eyeing number thirty-four with trepidation. He had heard the details of Madison's and Thompson's visit to Mrs Kaufman, and after watching her at the Shabbat service he determined that, given a choice, she would be the last person he would wish to visit.

Eventually, Brodmann got out of the car. He locked it carefully and started climbing up the drive leading to the house. It was not a very steep drive, but Brodmann was not very young and, he had to admit to himself, not very fit. At his age he no longer looked to have much action as a police officer. Office work and early retirement were how he saw his future in the force. But he liked working with Madison. They had bonded almost as soon as they met and with the years, and particularly after Madison lost his wife, the bond grew stronger. It was never something that was evident to anyone working with them. It was something they felt and understood, never actually defining it in words.

'Sooner done sooner mended,' Brodmann told himself as he reached the front door. He was intending to stop for a few seconds in order to take three or four deep breaths before ringing the doorbell, but one deep breath was all he managed as the door opened to reveal Mrs Kaufman in all her intimidating persona.

'Can I help you?' she demanded.

The woman had a knack of taking anyone and everyone out of their comfort zone.

Brodmann fished into his pockets – the damned card was never in the first pocket he searched – and found his warrant card on the third try.

'Sergeant Brodmann, Mrs Kaufman,' he said, while presenting her with the card. 'Could I come in?'

'Brodmann?' Mrs Kaufman enquired. 'I knew a Brodmann once. What was his name... yes... Paul. Paul Brodmann. Any relation?'

'Well, I do have a brother and his name is Paul...'

'Is he a doctor?' Mrs Kaufman continued.

'As a matter of fact, yes, he is,' Brodmann said. He was still standing at the door with no sign of being invited to enter.

'Well, that must be awkward for you, Sergeant,' Mrs Kaufman said.

Mrs Kaufman could always put her finger on the point – and tact was never her strongest trait.

As a child, Brodmann had dreamt of being a policeman and he never grew out of it – possibly until now. His younger brother, the doctor, was clearly more successful, much richer, enjoyed grand holidays – and to top it all, it was impossible to hate him, as Paul loved his brother, his sister-in-law, his nephews and nieces. Brodmann loved his brother but that didn't stop him resenting him a little.

His annoyance gave Brodmann courage.

'Shall we continue inside, Mrs Kaufman?' he said, and walked in as Mrs Kaufman opened the door wider.

'Would you like a cup of tea?'

Brodmann thought he heard wrongly.

'Pardon?'

'I asked if you would like a cup of tea,' Mrs Kaufman repeated.

Brodmann decided not to tell the chief inspector about this invitation. Knowing Madison, he might send him to visit Mrs Kaufman daily.

'That would be very nice. Thanks.'

Mrs Kaufman led Brodmann into the room she called the snug. This was the room she and Mr Kaufman used to sit in of an evening, watch television, read and occasionally even talk to each other.

Although he did not know this, Brodmann was honoured to be invited into this room. Very few visitors were ever allowed into 'the snug'.

While Mrs Kaufman was out getting the tea, Brodmann surveyed the room. After twenty-five years in the police, he was in the habit, almost without realising he did it, of studying any environment he found himself in and filing the information in his head.

The room was very tidy and clean. Minimally furnished, making it look quite roomy. There were very few ornaments on display but each one of them looked expensive.

There were a few pictures on the wall. Brodmann stood up and studied each one. They were all signed but the names were not familiar to Brodmann, which did not mean a lot, as he would not consider himself an art connoisseur.

He noticed that there were no family photos on display.

The carpet was off-white. Brodmann was surprised he was not asked to take his shoes off. The three-piece suite was grey with a touch of silver leather. The room felt cold. The Kaufmans clearly did not do warm and cosy.

If he was asked to describe the room in one word, Brodmann would say 'pretentious'.

Brodmann got back to his seat on the sofa just as Mrs Kaufman entered the room, rolling a trolley with drinks and what looked like cake on it.

Brodmann was surprised. He fully expected a reception such as the chief inspector and Lisa Thompson described.

'How do you take your tea, Sergeant?' Mrs Kaufman asked.

16

DCI Madison popped his head through the door of the synagogue's office. The two secretaries looked up from their computers.

Becky Mosco smiled and said, 'Good morning, Chief Inspector. How can we help you?'

Madison noticed that Jane Barker stared at him but left the talking to her assistant.

Madison stepped into the office and directed his words to Jane Barker.

'I was hoping you could join me in the incident room, Miss Barker?'

'What… now?'

Lisa Thompson was right. Miss Barker was scared and Madison wanted to find out what of.

'That would be good,' Madison replied.

'But… I am working. I have to finish this before tonight. Can it wait?'

Madison awarded Jane Barker one of his special smiles, preserved for the very nervous witnesses.

'It won't take long, Miss Barker, and I'm afraid it has to be now. This is a murder investigation.'

Jane's face, usually of pale complexion, now looked almost white. She stood up and followed the chief inspector to what used to be the caretaker's room and now was a small but very impressive incident room.

Lisa Thompson was sitting at the other side of the table, a notebook and pen in her hand.

'This is PC Lisa Thompson.' Madison pointed in Lisa's direction. 'I think you two have already met. Lisa will be taking notes. Can I get you a cup of coffee or tea?'

'No, thanks. I really have to get back… to work.'

'I understand,' Madison said, sitting down and inviting her to do the same. He was amused by the way she sat – so much like Brodmann did at the Shabbat service.

'You are right, Miss Barker. Let's get right to the point. The sooner we start the sooner you can get back to your work. Now – I hear that you were one of Mr Kaufman's strongest supporters.'

'Who told you that?'

'I am told you always voted with Mr Kaufman during board meetings. In fact, was it not you who proposed Mr Kaufman for the chair position?'

'Yes, but… that doesn't mean…'

'You were good friends with Mr Kaufman?'

'No. I was not.'

'So – if you were not friendly with Mr Kaufman, you must have had a lot of respect for him?'

'I did not. I don't know where you are getting all this. People gossip… you shouldn't listen to everything they say…'

Madison was not going to tell Miss Barker that he got his information from the rabbi. She was nervous enough without knowing that.

'That is precisely why I am asking you, Miss Barker,' he replied. 'I want you to tell me why you were such a supporter of Mr Kaufman if you neither liked nor respected him?'

'I didn't say I didn't like him,' Miss Barker protested. 'You are putting words in my mouth.'

'I am really sorry. I don't wish to do that. So – you did like him?'

'I didn't say that either. Why are you questioning me like that? Are you saying… Am I a suspect?'

'Now, Miss Barker – you are putting words in my mouth. That is not what I'm saying.'

'So why all the questions?'

'Because, Miss Barker, you did support Mr Kaufman from the moment he joined the board of the synagogue. I understand you were the only one who supported him a hundred percent of the time. I need to know why. You say you were not friends; you did not even respect him – yet you must have had full confidence in his ability to do the job. Can you explain this to me?'

At this point Miss Barker burst into tears, taking the vastly experienced chief inspector by surprise. He sat for a while, watching her sobbing hysterically, not quite sure how to react. He made a mental note to ask PC Benson to make sure they had some tissues in the incident room. There was absolutely nothing in the way of a paper towel or napkin to offer Miss Barker, but the resourceful Miss Thompson fished a couple of tissues from her bag and offered them to Miss Barker, who took them gratefully.

'Thank you,' she said through her tears. 'I have tissues… in my bag but… I left it in the office.'

'Don't worry about it,' Lisa said, and returned to her chair, picking up her notebook and resuming writing.

Miss Barker blew her nose and dabbed her eyes while murmuring, 'I'm sorry. I don't know what came over me… It's all been… very upsetting.'

Madison sat there, taking his time, giving her a chance to recover.

The silence in the room seemed to make her more unsettled. She kept murmuring things and Madison was happy to let her continue.

'I am a crier, always have been. The slightest thing gets me going. I'm sorry… but a murder… in the synagogue… it's awful.'

'It is not good,' Madison agreed. 'I have to admit it is my first one in a synagogue.'

Miss Barker looked up.

'Is it?' she asked, looking at the chief inspector hopefully, as if by sharing an experience, he would go easy on her.

'Miss Barker,' Madison said, awarding her with his warmest smile, 'I am not the enemy. I am not here to hurt you – unless, of course, you are the one who… pushed Mr Kaufman…'

'I didn't!' she cried. 'I wouldn't… couldn't, even if I wanted to.'

'Did you want to?'

Miss Barker looked at the chief inspector for a moment and then said softly, 'Sometimes… yes. Sometimes I did. But I could never…'

Madison fixed his eye on her and did not speak, waiting for her to continue.

Lisa looked up from her notebook and gave Miss Barker a supportive little smile.

'Mr and Mrs Kaufman joined the synagogue when I was in my fifth year as a secretary. I was happy in the job, but I didn't have any social contacts with anyone here. I guess secretaries don't… and not being Jewish myself… well, I never expected to be socially accepted. But when the Kaufmans arrived, they befriended me, which was nice. They were really interested in me and invited me over for dinner a few times. Then one time I was invited for Friday dinner… I don't drink, but they opened a very special bottle which they kept for special occasions… and I agreed to have a little, just being polite. Then they filled my glass again and… well, not being used to drinking, I ended up being quite sick and they drove me home. I was so embarrassed. I couldn't apologise enough… their special bottle ending up in their loo…'

Madison and Lisa smiled in sympathy.

'We have all been there, Miss Barker.'

'Well – not me… not before. I just don't drink normally…'

Miss Barker looked up at the chief inspector.

'I think I will have that cup of tea after all, Chief Inspector. My throat is so dry…'

Lisa jumped off her chair and busied herself boiling the kettle and getting the cups down.

'Jack—gov. Tea?'

'Yes, please,' Madison replied, still looking at Miss Barker.

For a while only the sound of the kettle boiling could be heard.

Madison allowed Miss Barker a few sips of her tea. He tried not to betray his impatience.

Miss Barker looked up from her cup and must have sensed it as she continued hurriedly.

'I'm sorry. This is so hard… Anyhow, when the time came to elect a new chair for the board, he came to me and asked if I would propose him for the position. I am on the board – not because I was elected or anything, but because I am the secretary. I write the minutes and send them out… that sort of thing… Anyhow, I was surprised because Cecil – Mr Kaufman – only joined the board the previous year. I told him I tried to stay out of synagogue's politics… I told him I was only writing the minutes…

Miss Barker stopped. She took another sip of her tea and blew her nose again.

'With a lovely smile on his face,' she continued, 'and a very soft and warm tone of voice, he let me know that he knew… he knew something that no one else knew… that I never wanted anyone else to know…'

17

She stands outside 992 like she had done so many times in the past, rolling the years back to her childhood, her teenage years, her twenties, and the forbidden love.

Number 992 is surrounded by beauty. Numbers 990 and 994 are shining in their restored magnificence. As are 988 and 996 and the rest. In the twenty-four years that had passed, they had all been loved, cherished, made up and lovingly restored. All but 992.

She slowly climbs the stairs leading to the entrance hall. The smell hits her nostrils. The same smell – unpleasant to most but to her – the smell of home. The peeling plaster on the walls. The broken stair – still the same. As if she walked away only yesterday.

She can almost hear the piano playing. Herself. Goldberg variations. That passage in 'Variation 8'. Again and again and again…

And then – the forbidden love.

She wipes a tear away and turns her back on 992. Till the next time.

18

'So, Dave – how did you get on with Mrs Kaufman?'

In spite of his determination not to divulge the information to Madison, Brodmann just could not help himself.

'All I can say is,' he started, allowing himself a little cheeky smile, 'that reports of a superb lemon drizzle were not exaggerated.'

Madison and Lisa looked up at Brodmann in amazement.

'She offered you cake?' Madison could not hide his astonishment.

'Sent some home with me for my wife to taste.' Brodmann was enjoying the effect his words had on the three officers.

'Mrs Kaufman?' Madison was incredulous. 'Are you sure you went to the right house?'

'Mrs Kaufman, Yes. The same.'

'Just because you are Jewish?'

'Well… not just… My brother, the doctor, had something to do with it.'

'What about your brother the doctor?'

'He was the Kaufmans' doctor before they moved into this area.'

'I love lemon drizzle cake,' Lisa said, biting on her pencil. 'Did you not bring us some?'

'She specifically said for my wife and also for my brother.'

'The doctor wins again,' Madison said, teasingly. He knew all about the rivalry Brodmann had going with his doctor brother. 'So – while munching on a slice or two of lemon drizzle, did you manage to learn anything?'

Brodmann was glad of the opportunity to get off the subject of the cake. It was beginning to get uncomfortable.

'I did get something,' he said. 'They lived down south for most of their marriage but Cecil – Mr Kaufman – lost his job. I got the impression that it wasn't the first job he had lost and he wanted to get away. He had been in textiles or something. Everything was too expensive down south, so he managed to find a job with a family relative up in Manchester, also in textiles. Mrs Kaufman hates it up here and she hates belonging to the reform synagogue.'

'Why did they not join the Orthodox one?'

'His new boss belongs to the reform synagogue and he suggested they join. Also, I think Mr Kaufman thought he had more chance of rising to the top of the board at the reform synagogue. He wasn't really "kosher" enough for the Orthodox Jews…'

'So she looks down on all these reform Jews?' Madison smirked. 'A bit like you, really?'

'Well, yes. I happen to agree with her – to a point. It's neither here nor there… They seem to be playing at being good Jews by picking up the bits they like and dropping the bits that are more difficult.'

'And that is worse than dropping just about all of it while still criticising those who are keeping some of it?' Madison demanded.

'Jack… with respect… I don't really want to have this discussion with you.'

'That's fine... you clearly have more in common with Mrs Kaufman than with me!'

In the silence that followed, only PC Benson was heard stirring a little sugar into his cup.

'So,' Madison continued after a pause, 'she basically hated being here and hates everyone attending this synagogue.'

'More or less. She hates the rabbi mostly. Some scandal apparently. Completely unsuitable to lead, et cetera. She can't forgive the congregation for voting her husband off the chair position. You would think it was the US elections. Intrigues, conspiracies, hate campaign... to be honest, I'd had enough for one visit, so I said I needed to be back here for four. There is only so much a man can take.'

'And,' Madison continued his friend's sentence, 'you knew that, after the rapport you seem to have established with the woman, I was bound to be sending you back there.'

'Quite.' Brodmann stood up and went for the kettle. PC Benson had made it clear that, from day two, it was each to him or her own with refreshments. He was a policeman, he said. Not a waiter.

'I am not sure what to make of this yet, but it's early days. OK, Benson... sorry, Josh. Is it short for Joshua?'

'It is, yes. I don't like being called Joshua. Too biblical.'

'Indeed,' Madison said, looking intently at PC Benson. As yet, the young policeman was a closed book to him. Apart from his obvious tidiness and flair for the domestic, Madison knew very little about PC Benson.

'So, Josh – did you manage to speak to the caretaker?'

'I did, sir, yes – sorry, Jack – he is a character... an avid reader. We spent half of the interview discussing whether the film or BBC series of *Pride and Prejudice* better reflected the book. He's read all of Jane Austen's novels, Oscar Wilde's writing, he speaks three languages and—'

'Slow down, Benson.' Madison interrupted the flow of reporting. 'This is fascinating, but did you get any time to ask him about the day of the murder?'

'Of course I did, Jack.' Benson proudly remembered to address Madison by his first name. 'He was working most of the day on building a shed in the front garden of the synagogue. Came in only to get a drink and visit the loo. I spoke briefly to the two secretaries and they confirmed this. I ascertained that no one can come in or out of the synagogue without the two secretaries seeing them. Even people who have the keys to the building – board members, Rabbi and so – have to walk past the office window to get to the entrance door. The two ladies never take a break at the same time so that, while the synagogue is open, no one can come in unnoticed.'

'Well done, Josh,' Madison said. 'Can you write a report in the evidence book so we can all read it?'

'Will do. There's one more thing… about Jonson.'

'Oh, yes?'

'Well… he has a theory.'

'Theory?'

'I think he fancies himself as a bit of a psychologist. Amateur, of course. He thinks Mr Kaufman jumped.'

Three pairs of eyes looked at Benson in surprise.

'Yes, he thinks Kaufman killed himself. He says that the vote to remove him from chair of the synagogue was the last straw. He had been sacked before. Jonson thinks he was depressed. He had nothing to live for… no children, no grandchildren, no job, and now forced to vacate the chair position.'

'Interesting…' Madison had a glint in his eye. To those who knew him, it would be obvious that a cheeky remark was about to be delivered. 'So depressed, in fact, that he first bashed himself on the head, and then jumped?'

'Well… I didn't tell Jonson that he was bashed on the head

before going down. I didn't think I had the authority to tell him that.'

'You did the right thing, Josh.' Madison was beginning to think that Benson would prove to be a good addition to his team. 'Lisa, anything to report? I know I took most of your afternoon with Miss Barker, but did you manage to talk to Miss Mosco?'

'I did manage a short interview with Becky. She hates being called Miss Mosco. Asked me to call her Becky. Anyhow – she is a lot of fun. Giggles a lot. Not in a nervous way. I got the impression she genuinely sees the funny side in everything.'

'Everything? Even murder at the synagogue?'

'No. Not that. But that didn't stop her from being frank about Mr Kaufman and his wife.'

Madison smiled.

'Does she also have a theory about the murderer?'

'To quote Becky accurately, she actually said, "I would happily have throttled him myself!"'

'Did she? Well, that must take her out of the list of suspects.'

'I must say – I would be really upset if it turns out to be her. I really liked her.

'She wouldn't comment on any members of the synagogue,' Lisa added. 'Clearly more than her job is worth. So, apart from confirming that no one can enter without them seeing them and confirming the list of people who visited the synagogue on the day, she was not much of a help.'

Madison was quiet for a moment.

'So, both secretaries can see whoever comes in, but what happens if, say, one of them has to go to the loo?'

'They never go at the same time,' Lisa answered. 'They take turns.'

'I understand.' Madison continued. 'But if they don't go

together, that means that for the duration of the loo visit, neither of them has an alibi.'

The room went silent while the three were considering this remark.

'I see what you mean,' Lisa said at last, 'but surely, going to the loo doesn't give you enough time to go to the synagogue hall, climb up to the balcony, do the deed and then come out and return to the office.'

'That would depend on whether you were having a short or a long stop at the loo,' Madison insisted. 'After all, you wouldn't be timing your colleague's toilet break, would you? Sometimes people take quite a long time to relieve themselves – enough time to do exactly that.'

'But,' Benson quibbled, 'the murderer – if it was one of the secretaries – would have no way of knowing how long the other one was going to spend in the loo.'

'That's true,' Lisa agreed. 'Although, often when people rely on each other for having their toilet breaks, one might say something like, "I'm going to be quite a while." Or, "I won't be a minute." So in that way, they might have given each other an idea of how long they would be.'

'Possibly,' Madison said.

'Do you want us to find out if either of the secretaries went to the loo before Mr Kaufman's body was found?' Benson did not look as if he fancied taking on this job.

'We might have to. As a matter of fact, we might have to ask if the rabbi and the caretaker also had a toilet break. The rabbi could come out of his room, go to the toilet – or anywhere else in the building – and come back without the secretaries knowing about it.'

The room was silent for a few minutes while everyone was considering these options.

'So, I think at this stage we can't disregard anyone. In

certain circumstances, they all had opportunities to murder Mr Kaufman. We have to establish the motive first. We have to interview all of them again.'

'Jack,' Lisa said. 'What about Miki Solomon? We haven't mentioned her at all.'

'Ah, yes. Miss Solomon. I don't think we need to worry about her going to the loo. She didn't stay long enough, but yes. We need to talk to her too. Unfortunately, she is away on tour. Apparently went to the airport straight from her visit to the synagogue. Wanted her music with her. Can you check and confirm she is back on Wednesday, Lisa?'

'Will do.'

'At this stage,' Madison continued, 'anything is possible and everyone is a possible suspect, which brings me to Miss Barker. The secretary. Very interesting. Lisa was quite right, sensing Miss Barker was hiding something. As it happens, something very big. Lisa – would you like to give us the basic story there while I refresh my cup of tea?'

Lisa was a little taken aback at this but recovered quickly.

'Well,' she said, standing up, 'it seems that the Kaufmans befriended her from the moment they joined the synagogue. Invited her for meals and things, and on one occasion poured so much wine down her throat – not literally, you know – that she was sick and remembered very little about it. It was only later, when Mr Kaufman wanted her to propose him for the chair position, that he revealed he knew things about her.'

Madison returned to his chair with a fresh cup of tea and took over.

'Apparently, in her drunken state – she doesn't normally drink – she answered questions she would never have answered otherwise. She gave in and proposed him and has been supporting him ever since for fear of him exposing her.'

'What was the big secret?' Benson asked.

'As yet we don't know. She was in quite a state and I left it for the time being. But this is crucial information. She has no memory of what happened and is worried she might have given them more information. Secretaries, in my experience, know everything about the institution they work for, and I wouldn't be surprised if she supplied the Kaufmans with valuable blackmail material.

'So, it seems obvious that Mr Kaufman had information on one or more of our suspects. We need to find out who and why.'

In the silence that followed, Benson asked, 'If that is the case, Jack' – he dropped the name very carefully, still feeling uncomfortable using it – 'doesn't it follow that Mrs Kaufman too might be in danger?'

Madison looked at the young policeman with renewed interest.

'You will make a fine detective, Josh,' Madison said. 'I have started worrying about that too. Can you arrange a patrol unit to look after Mrs Kaufman's house? But she must not spot them. I don't think she would take kindly to it. I am making a return visit to Mrs Kaufman. Dave – you are coming with me. I need you for protection.'

19

Jon Jonson was impressed.

'This is amazing,' he said, looking around what used to be his cramped office-cum-hidey-hole-cum-cleaning room. 'How did you do this in such a short time?'

'All credit to PC Benson,' Madison said. 'He is very industrious. Half an hour in his company and you will be exhausted.'

'I hardly recognise my little room,' Jon said, moving around and touching things. 'Do you think I can keep some of these things when you are done?'

'I assume it is all police property, but I will see what I can do,' Madison said. 'Do sit down.'

Jon Jonson sat down facing Madison, but his eyes were still wandering around the room.

'PC Benson tells me that you have an interesting take on the death of Mr Kaufman?'

'Well – I'm no expert, Chief Inspector.'

'No, but I am still interested to know where your theory is coming from. Did you know Mr Kaufman well?'

'I wasn't a bosom friend, if that's what you mean, Chief Inspector, but I did some work for the Kaufmans when they first moved into the area. Little jobs in the house that needed doing, you know. Leaking taps, cupboard doors that hang loose… that sort of thing. So I spent quite a few hours in the house and had chats with both Mr and Mrs Kaufman – although I have to admit that Mrs Kaufman was quite snooty and making small talk with the caretaker of the synagogue wasn't something she approved of. But Mr Kaufman – when she was out of the house – was quite talkative. I thought he was depressed. She used to put him down all the time, even in front of me…'

'Put him down?' Madison asked. 'How? What about?'

'Well, I got the impression money was tight. He had lost his job down south, which is why they came up here. She was quite upset about that… He was working but not on a permanent basis… freelance… When I was there, he was often free to come and check what I was doing and talk to me. He liked talking!

'I definitely think she was the boss, you know? And she didn't like it up north. She kept referring to her family and "social group" which was down south…'

'So, you think Mr Kaufman jumped off that balcony. Surely, if he wanted to kill himself, there would be easier ways of doing it?' Madison didn't betray the fact that they now knew Mr Kaufman was hit on the head before he fell.

'I'm sure I don't know, Chief Inspector. I'm just guessing. I just thought… He wasn't a very happy man…'

'Did you see Mr Kaufman on the day he died?' Madison enquired. 'Did you speak to him?'

'I did. When he came in. I was working outside on the shed and he said hello and asked how I was doing, the usual kind of thing.'

'How did he seem to you?'

'I don't really know… I wasn't paying a lot of attention. I was really busy putting up the shed. He seemed quite normal.'

'You have a key to the building, right?'

'It's not really a key. It's a fob. But sure, I have one.'

'So, you can come and go without needing the secretaries to open the door for you?'

'I can… What are you getting at, Chief Inspector?'

'Mr Jonson, I'm sure you appreciate that I need to ask these questions.'

'Yes but… I already told your officer that I was outside practically all day.'

'Practically?'

'Well, the odd cup of tea…'

'And a toilet break?'

'That too, but…'

'And as you let yourself in and out of the building, it doesn't follow that the secretaries would have seen you letting yourself in and going to the toilet?'

Mr Jonson was getting visibly angry.

'I don't use the synagogue's toilet. I go home when I need to…'

'Really? How far is home?'

'I thought you knew. I live at the back of the synagogue.'

Madison froze.

'You live at the back of the synagogue? How come I didn't know that?'

'I don't know. Everybody knows where I live. Can't tell you how many times people come knocking at the door, wanting something from the synagogue when it is closed…'

Madison stood up. He looked angry.

'Right. Let's go there.'

'Go where?'

'Your house, of course. Where did you think?'

'But I'm working. I can't just go home.'

'Yes, you can. We can inform the office on the way out.'

20

Madison stood in the back garden of Jonson's house. The garden was bordered by a living fence, and quite well concealed within that border was a gate that opened into the back garden of the synagogue.

'I assume this is how you go to work? Through this gate?'

Madison was trying to keep his tone of voice down.

'Yes, it is…'

Jonson could sense that the chief inspector was unhappy, but was not sure what he had done wrong.

'And who else can get to the synagogue through this gate without being seen by the office?'

'No one. Just me.'

'Mr Jonson – I and my team have spent three days questioning all the people who came into the building, according to the secretaries. At no point was I told that there is a way in without being seen by the secretaries.'

'Chief Inspector, I'm sorry you didn't know about it. It never occurred to me you didn't know – but I assure you, no one can get through here without my knowing about it.'

Jonson walked around his garden with Madison following.

'As you can see, there is no way into the back garden except through the house. The house is locked and the alarm is on – as you saw.'

'Who else has a key to your house, Mr Jonson?'

'My daughter, Chief Inspector. She is in London.'

'What about neighbours? Don't you have a key with a neighbour in case your alarm goes?'

'Oh, yes… sorry, Chief Inspector. I clean forgot. Mr Adams, the next-door neighbour. He is a friend.'

'Does he belong to this synagogue?' Madison asked, his face stern.

'What? No. He belongs to the Methodist church at the top of the street. We both do.'

'Has he ever been to the synagogue?'

'Stewart? I don't know… why would he?'

'I am asking you that, Mr Jonson.'

'Now listen here, Chief Inspector. I've had enough of this. What exactly are you accusing me of here?'

'I am not accusing you of anything, Mr Jonson.' Madison knew he was taking his frustration out on the caretaker. Somehow, he and his team failed to find out that the caretaker's house opened directly into the synagogue's grounds. 'I apologise if I made it sound as if I was accusing you. We have been assuming that the only way into the synagogue was via the main entrance. I don't know how I missed it before. I walked all around the synagogue…'

Jonson, now feeling a little more relaxed, answered with a certain degree of pride. 'You can't really see the gate from the synagogue side. I did that deliberately. Worrying about my privacy, to be honest. It's practically camouflaged. It's more about the children, you know. They often play ball out here during the service and I wasn't going to have them running in and out of my garden every time they lost a ball. The gate is locked but that wouldn't stop them trying to open it if they saw the gate.'

Jonson moved ahead of Madison and unlocked the gate. He pointed to the side door of the synagogue.

'This door is always locked,' he said. 'If by any chance anyone came into the grounds of the synagogue through my garden, they would still have to go to the front entrance if they wanted to go into the synagogue, as this door is always locked. It only ever opens when we need to bring things – furniture, et cetera – into the synagogue. Otherwise, it is always closed.'

Madison considered this for a while.

'Who has the key to this door?'

'Same people who have the key to the front door. Myself, the rabbi, the secretary and a couple of board members – usually the chair and one more member.'

'Well… thank you, Mr Jonson,' Madison said, walking towards the gate. 'That will be all for the time being. You were very helpful.'

21

'I felt like such a fool,' Madison said to his team as they all assembled in the incident room. 'How come we all missed the fact that the caretaker's house was behind the synagogue and opened into the grounds?'

'You would think someone would have mentioned it,' Benson said.

Brodmann was not so sure.

'Why would they? From what Jonson said, no one ever walked through the gate apart from himself, so it probably never even occurred to them.'

'From what Jonson said!' Madison said, rather loudly. 'From what Jonson said. I don't want to rely on what Jonson – or anyone else – said. They could all be lying. We need to rely on facts, not on what people say which they can't support with evidence.'

The little room went silent for a while.

'It probably means that we have to widen the list of suspects,' Lisa said finally.

'Exactly that,' Madison answered. 'We can no longer assume that only the people who entered and left by the front door are suspects.'

'Does that mean we now have to question Jonson's neighbour too?' Benson wondered.

'It means that and more.' Madison stood up and walked to the small window through which he could see the well 'camouflaged' gate to the caretaker's house. 'But before starting on the neighbour, I have to really lay into Miss Barker. We now need to know every single secret about the congregation she might, in her drunken state, have betrayed to the Kaufmans. I will do that first. In the meantime, I want you, Dave, to talk to Jonson. A fresh approach might get more results. I'm afraid I was so angry when I realised his house could have been used for the murder that I lost any subtlety I might have possessed. Try to get out of him any information he might have thought too insignificant to mention, but at the same time keep remembering that he might have deliberately chosen not to tell us something. I am convinced that his house plays a part in this matter. I don't know why. It's just a feeling.'

22

DAY 7

Sergeant Brodmann helped himself to two cups of coffee before dragging himself out to face Jonson, who was still working on the shed outside.

Brodmann had not had a good night. Although he tried to shake off work problems when coming home to his family, Brodmann could not get the image of Cecil Kaufman lying at the foot of the Torah cupboard out of his mind. He even visited that scene in his dreams, which really worried him. He was always determined that work stayed at work. Dave had been through many murder cases and was always able to take a break from them when home with the family. This case, though, was getting to him on so many levels. The body lying across the Holy of Holies; referring to this cupboard, in this synagogue, as Holy of Holies; his Jewishness suddenly becoming part of the investigation; Madison mocking his attitude to this synagogue.

Brodman drank the last drop of his second cup of coffee and walked out to where Jonson was busy building a shed. He stood there for a while, watching Jonson at work before speaking.

'That's first-class work, Mr Jonson,' Brodmann said, and meant it.

Jonson turned around, saw who it was and turned back to his work, saying nothing.

'My father was good at making and building things,' Brodmann said. 'I'm afraid I haven't inherited his talent.'

'It's nothing to do with talent,' Jonson muttered. 'It's a matter of something needing doing.'

Brodmann let this go. His wife long ago forbade him from mending anything around the house. It was cheaper, she claimed, to get the professionals in right from the start.

Jonson carried on working in silence for a while and Brodmann was happy to wait.

'So, what is it this time, Officer?' Jonson said at last. 'Have you come to arrest me?'

'Arrest you? What gave you that idea?'

'Your boss did!'

'I'm sorry about that. The chief inspector was taken aback when he discovered—'

'Well, it's not my fault that I live behind the synagogue. If I knew the trouble it would get me into, I would have got a house somewhere else.'

'You are really not in any trouble, Mr Jonson. The chief inspector wouldn't want you to think that.'

'Really? I would hate to be there when he does want someone to think they are in trouble.'

'Mr Jonson, believe me. The chief inspector regrets how he spoke to you. That's why he asked me to—'

'If he is really sorry, Officer, shouldn't he be saying it to me himself, rather than sending you to do his dirty job?'

Brodmann could not really argue with that point. He also wished Madison had talked to Jonson himself. As Jonson returned to working on the shed, Brodmann watched in silence for a while.

'You do understand, Mr Jonson,' he said at last, 'that the chief inspector cannot ignore this revelation that there is another way into the synagogue that the office cannot monitor.'

Jonson turned to look at Brodmann.

'But I told him – no one comes this way. I am the only one who uses this way to enter the synagogue. He clearly doesn't believe me.'

'Mr Jonson – can I call you Jon? Calling everyone Mr, Miss or Mrs can get quite tiring…' Brodmann took the silence as an agreement and continued. 'Jon, you have to understand. We are not allowed to just believe people. You are probably right that no one but you ever uses your garden to enter the synagogue, but it could be – just could be – that someone did. You can't ignore this possibility.'

'I don't see who could possibly…'

'Your neighbour could. I'm sure he didn't, but he could. This "could" element means we have to investigate it. You get it?'

Jon looked down at his shoes and it was clear that, in spite of himself, he was starting to see the point.

'We will have to talk to your neighbour, Jon. You can see that. And to your daughter.'

Jonson nodded.

'So, if you can please give me your daughter's telephone number and your neighbour's address… and please, Jon, think carefully if there is anyone at all who might have had access to your house – your garden – at any time. Someone might have – it's unlikely, but someone could… someone just could…'

23

She climbs the stairs and stands still for a while, taking in the familiar smell and sight. After a while she takes a path to the side of the building and walks outside the rooms that were once her life. It is dark and she hopes no one can see her. Standing in the back yard, she touches the wall of her room, so long ago. She closes her eyes and she is back there, in her room, on her bed where only the moment matters. The dangerous, forbidden love feels so right, so natural. She gives herself to it again, standing outside in the dark, her hand touching the wall of the room where things that should not have happened, happened.

24

'Miss Barker,' Madison said in a voice which clearly meant business. 'Please take a seat.'

Madison waited till Miss Barker sat down, then continued.

'You never mentioned that your caretaker lives at the back of the synagogue and that his garden opens into the synagogue's grounds.'

Miss Barker looked up in genuine surprise.

'You didn't know?' she asked. 'Everyone knows that. It never occurred to me…'

She was beginning to get upset.

'Are you saying that I deliberately didn't tell you?'

'What I am saying, Miss Barker, is that from now on I want you to tell me everything. Everything you know. Even if you think I already know it. You know more about the ins and outs of this synagogue than anyone else and I need you to talk to me.'

'I didn't… I wasn't hiding anything… I answered all your questions.'

'Well – this time, Miss Barker, there are going to be more questions and more answers. I want you to think carefully and tell me who else you might have told the Kaufmans about when you were there for dinner. What other confidential information do you have about other members of the synagogue that you might have unknowingly talked about on that night?'

'Can you please call me Jane, Chief Inspector?' Miss Barker said, suddenly sounding so much more confident. 'No one calls me Miss Barker. I hate the name. I divorced Mr Barker seven years ago and I'm only keeping the name for my daughter's sake, so please, drop the Miss.'

The transformation was astonishing. Suddenly, resenting her ex-husband's name, she became a lot more assertive.

'Sure,' Madison said. 'Jane is fine with me.'

'And to answer your question, Chief Inspector' – it was not lost on Madison that she emphasised the words 'Chief Inspector', suggesting he might also allow her to use his first name. He ignored it.

'I can't think of anyone else I might know something about which is… not known generally…' Jane concluded.

'How about Becky Mosco?'

'What about Becky?' Jane seemed really surprised.

'You must know her very well. You spend practically all day together in that office.'

'The office is a very busy place. People come in and out. It's not as if…'

'Are you friends with Becky?'

'We are friendly. We don't socialise or anything like that but we get on.'

'And talk about things? … All those hours in that little room, just the two of you…'

'Like I said – people come and go.'

'What do you talk about when it is just the two of you?'

'Oh, God – I don't know.'

'Did you tell her any information about anyone in the synagogue? Anything you might have told the Kaufmans also?'

'Absolutely not!' Jane was getting angry. 'These are things I am told in strict confidence. I don't go gossiping about them!'

'Not unless you have had a glass or two…'

Madison could see the hurt in her eyes and immediately took it back.

'I'm sorry. That was nasty. Please forgive me.'

Jane looked up at him.

'What's to forgive? I will never forgive myself for what happened that night…'

'If, that night, you talked about Becky at all, what do you think you might have said?'

'I don't really know… Not much to say. She is worried about money.'

'Yes?'

'Nothing major. Her husband lost his job. They don't have a lot in the way of savings… That sort of thing. Nothing more.'

Madison took a couple of minutes to digest what he had just heard.

'You say you don't socialise with Becky?'

'Not really. Occasionally we might nip out to get a sandwich at lunchtime – we would close the synagogue for a short break – but that would be twenty minutes or so and back to the office. We both prefer to work through and get home a little earlier.'

'And you never go out in the evenings with anyone from the synagogue?'

'Not really. Only for work.'

'For work?'

'I mean – if we are working on a certain project, we might meet in someone's house or occasionally over coffee somewhere more pleasant than the office.'

'You mean – Becky?'

'No, not Becky. Sometimes the rabbi, sometimes the chair… Oh – and before concerts I would occasionally meet with Miki.'

'Miki?'

'Miki Solomon. She was the head of music, before she resigned.'

Madison consulted his notes.

'Miki Solomon… she is abroad right now. Right?'

'Yes. She is back on Wednesday.'

'And you met over coffee to talk about some concerts?'

'Yes. She works big. There are a lot of organisations involved…'

'So, you have coffee… maybe some cake… and you talk only about the concerts?'

Jane smiled.

'Mostly…'

'And what do you talk about when it's not about the concerts?'

'Well, not much… I think I might have grumbled about Jeff – my ex, you know. I think she probably gave me a nudge when I was too scared to stand up to him.'

'So, you are friendly, if you felt like talking to her about it.'

'She is nice. Very easy to talk to.'

'And did she find you easy to talk to also?'

'I don't know… I hope so.'

'Did she pour her heart out to you too?'

At this point Jane went quiet. She felt she had talked too much. Madison's apology had broken down her barriers.

Madison realised this and said, gently, 'You are not betraying her confidence. You will be doing your duty – helping the police find out who killed Mr Kaufman.'

'But what could this possibly have to do with the murder? It was a good many months ago and just two women… talking to each other?'

'I can't answer that question, Jane, unless you tell me what you talked about. It could be that it had nothing to do with it, and it could be important.'

'It's really nothing,' Jane said at last. 'She just told me about something that happened a long time ago, when she was still living in Israel…'

Madison said nothing but looked at her intently, letting her know he was not letting her off the subject.

'I was moaning about my ex. He was being so difficult about our daughter. He insists she comes to visit him… he never comes up north… I hate her travelling on her own… Anyhow, I said something about her being lucky not to have married, something like that. I couldn't understand why she was on her own. She is gorgeous. Half the synagogue is in love with her. She laughed when I said it and just dropped a remark about someone… back home… years ago… I really don't know anything about it. She just said… she referred to it as forbidden love.'

'Forbidden? How?'

I don't know. I didn't ask, that's all I know about it.'

'And she told you this before your dinner with the Kaufmans?'

'Long before. I don't think I thought about it for months… years even.'

'However,' Madison said, 'if you were asked about it while under the influence of alcohol, you might have remembered and talked about it.'

'Oh, God… I'm sure I didn't. I hope I didn't… Oh, God.'

'What?' Madison could sense something else had occurred to her.

'She has been… different… for a while. Not as open. I thought, maybe? If Cecil said something about it to her, she would know it came from me. That's awful. What she must think of me…'

‘Miki has been avoiding you?’

‘I’m not sure. Thinking back… I mean, I haven’t really seen her since she resigned. Apart from that morning, when she came in on her way to the airport. I didn’t think much about it at the time because she was in a hurry. But now I’m thinking… if Cecil told her what I said… if I said it… that would explain why she never spoke to me when she came in. Only to Becky.’

Madison was taking in the information Miss Barker just revealed. It would seem that the mysterious Miki Solomon was also a victim of the Kaufmans’ blackmail operation – which, if true, would give her a motive for giving Cecil Kaufman a push off the balcony. But that still didn’t explain what Mr Kaufman was doing up on the balcony. His wife was adamant he never went up there, and all the other witnesses confirmed it.

‘Chief Inspector,’ Miss Barker said, mistaking his reveries for sudden loss of confidence. ‘Would this be all? I really must get back…’

Madison wanted to sort things out in his head before continuing the questioning.

‘It is not all,’ he replied, ‘but it is all for this minute. We will continue later.’

Miss Barker stood up. She knew very well that it was only a matter of time before he would force her secret out of her, but for the moment she was relieved to escape.

25

DAY 8

'We are getting nowhere,' Madison declared to his assembled team. 'If anything, the more we find out, the more complicated it gets. We thought we had a list of suspects and we were working our way through them when we discovered that, in fact, just about every member of this community or, in principle, any citizen of this country could, if he or she could get hold of a key, come in through Mr Jonson's garden.'

There was silence in the room. Madison's words did not surprise the team. He only expressed what they all knew – that they might have to start afresh.

Brodmann was the first to speak.

'I don't like bringing this up,' he started, sounding uncharacteristically hesitant.

'Bringing what up?' Madison asked impatiently. 'Come on, man. If it's relevant, we want to hear it. You don't need to like it.'

'I don't like it but I'm afraid it is relevant.'

Everyone in the room was looking at Brodmann in anticipation. It was not like the sergeant to speak in riddles.

'I really hope I am wrong, but I can't ignore the fact that it could have been an antisemitic attack on the synagogue.'

This speech was met with complete silence.

'My synagogue has had quite a few incidents. Swastikas on the synagogue's gate… threatening emails… even one break-in. While we were thinking it was an inside job, I was happy to ignore this possibility, but now that we are opening the investigation wider…'

'I can't believe I didn't think of it,' Madison said almost apologetically.

'It's like I said,' Brodmann continued, 'we had no reason to suspect anyone from outside the congregation – and I don't really seriously think that it was a hate crime. Someone would have to have intimate knowledge of the synagogue and the access from Jon's garden to have done this. I just think we need to keep this in mind.'

'I agree,' Madison replied. 'I will talk to the rabbi about it. I have to admit that it very much feels like an inside job, but I may well be wrong. Keep this in mind, everyone.'

Madison stopped as a thought occurred to him.

'Actually,' he said, 'there is one person who is, strictly speaking, outside the synagogue, but probably knows about Jon's garden and the access to the synagogue.'

'The neighbour?' Josh asked.

'Yes, Josh. The neighbour. He had the keys to the house. We need to talk to him.'

Madison looked at Josh. Then, as if he'd made up his mind, said, 'Josh, would you like to take this on?'

Josh was taken back.

'Sorry, gov… Jack.'

'Unless you think you are not up to it?' Madison challenged Benson.

'No… yes… I'm definitely up to it, Jack. I'm… thank you… I will.'

Madison smiled.

'Good. That's settled then.'

Brodmann checked his notes.

'The neighbour is Mr Adams. Mr Stewart Adams. I have his address here.'

Brodmann passed a piece of paper to Benson.

'It's the next house on the left,' Brodmann added.

'Thanks, Dave.' Madison turned back to Benson. 'Tell him it's routine. That you are talking to all the neighbours. I want to know if he knows anyone in the synagogue at all. Rabbi, chair – anyone. But try to do it subtly.'

Brodmann smiled but resisted making an easy jibe at Madison's failure in the subtlety department.

Madison was impressed with the young officer. If Benson came back from questioning the neighbour with some doubts, Madison would follow it up, but for now, it was only one of the avenues they had to explore. Madison still had a strong sense that the Kaufmans' penchant for blackmail must be the reason for the murder.

'In the meantime – Dave, how did you get on with Jonson?'

Brodmann smiled.

'It took a while. He was really angry with you. Cut me cold at first. I explained the situation and he seemed more placid by the end.'

'I will talk to him sometime. I shouldn't have taken it out on him. Did he have anything interesting to say?'

'Not really, Jack. He used to talk with Kaufman quite a bit while doing odd jobs for them. He thought Kaufman was really depressed. That being voted off the chairmanship was the last straw, after all the jobs he had lost. I didn't mention that he was hit before he fell. You could break this to him when you next talk to him.'

Madison ignored this dig at himself. He got up, took a last sip of his tea and rinsed the cup.

'I think it is time to see the rabbi again,' he said, turning around to face his team. 'I will do that presently. Lisa – I had a long session with Jane. I will fill you in on that conversation. But I did not yet hit her with the big question – what the Kaufmans had on her. She knows it is coming and was in a state. I think this would be better coming from a woman. If you could somehow tempt her away from the office, even from the building? Maybe suggest having coffee somewhere outside the synagogue? She might say no, in which case you will have to bring her back here, but I'd rather you didn't. See what you can do. If softly softly doesn't work, I will have to get tough with her.'

26

Lisa put her head through the office door.

'Hi,' she said. 'Sorry for bothering you. Is there any chance I can borrow a stapler?'

The two secretaries looked up and smiled.

'Sure,' Jane said, and picked up a stapler from her desk.

Lisa walked into the office and took the stapler that Jane was offering.

'Thank you so much. It's always a problem, moving the office from the police station to an incident room. Something is always missing… While I'm here, can you recommend a nice café where I can have a bite of lunch?'

Becky looked at Jane.

'There are few we go to sometimes. I think the one on the corner is probably our favourite… Jane?'

Jane agreed. 'The one on the corner. Yes. it is called Gabbi's. You can't miss it.'

'Thanks.' Lisa turned to leave the room, hesitated and turned back, facing Jane. 'You wouldn't fancy joining me, would you? It's just… I never feel right sitting on my own at a café or a restaurant…'

This little lie rolled off Lisa's tongue with the greatest of ease. *I have been in the job too long*, she said to herself. She was forever escaping the office on her lunch breaks and often walked further from the locals most of the policemen went to in order to get some time on her own.

Jane looked uncomfortable.

'I am working…'

'Me too.' Lisa smiled cheekily. 'But it is lunchtime and a girl has to eat. We won't be long.'

'Go on, Jane,' Becky said. 'I will hold the fort here – if you get me one of their nice croissant sandwiches.'

Jane was not fooled. She knew the policewoman wanted to quiz her further. She had been expecting it, but thought it would be the chief inspector doing the questioning. She would rather talk to this nice young woman.

'OK,' she said. 'But I must be back here by one thirty at the latest. I am expecting an important phone call.'

'No problem,' Lisa said. 'Thanks. I'll just put the stapler in the little room and join you.'

27

Again, Madison surprised himself at the ease with which he was conversing with Rabbi Zimmerman. On the face of it, the two men had nothing in common. Madison came from a Methodist family but, like most of his relatives, was very lax about his faith. He accepted that when he departed this world, he would probably have some sort of a Christian burial, but other than that he was quite happy to live a secular life. Strangely, though, Madison thought that, had he felt the need for spiritual guidance, he would be more likely to find it in this room.

Madison reminded himself that this man sitting opposite him, far from offering spiritual guidance, was one of his suspects in a murder case.

'How is the investigation coming on, Chief Inspector?' Zimmerman asked. 'Are you getting any nearer to a result?'

Madison allowed a little sigh to escape before answering.

'Every time I think we might be getting somewhere, something happens and I'm finding myself further from a resolution than ever.'

Madison immediately regretted saying that. It was almost as if he was in a virtual confession box. This man was dangerous.

Talking to him came so naturally that, if he wasn't careful, the chief inspector could find himself giving out information instead of taking some in.

'Rabbi,' he said, with renewed interest, 'what do you make of Jon Jonson?'

'Jon?' the rabbi asked, somewhat surprised. 'I was about to say I would trust him with my life, but that would be going over the top a little. But I do trust him. I think he is a very decent guy. Why? Do you think… you can't possibly think he did it?'

'As a member of a jury, you are always reminded that everyone is innocent unless proven guilty. As a police detective, though, you learn to think that everyone is guilty, unless proven innocent.'

'I understand that,' Rabbi Zimmerman said, almost in sympathy. 'But you asked me for my opinion and I tell you again – I have known him for years now and I think it would be hard to find a more decent man.'

'Even amongst your congregation?' Madison was feeling a lot more comfortable now that his inner detective slotted into place after a short relapse.

The rabbi smiled.

'I couldn't possibly comment,' he said.

'Fair enough,' Madison replied.

'People tend to think of a house of prayer as a place you come to, to be comforted and advised and get together with others, helping, grieving with them, celebrating with them. A place where the sun always shines. The fact is that it is an institution like all institutions, where human beings are shown at their best and at their worst. We are not "synagogue people". We are just people.'

On the basis of the few 'synagogue people' Madison had already met, he had to agree with the rabbi.

'Rabbi,' he asked, 'can you think of anyone else who might have had a grudge against Mr Kaufman? We have established that he was blackmailing some people in order to get them to support him, but there might be others who, for one reason or another, hated him.'

'There may have been, Chief Inspector, but I can't think of any.'

'Or you won't?'

'Chief Inspector,' Rabbi Zimmerman said, a sad look in his eyes, 'I am the rabbi of this community. I see my duty as trying to find and encourage the best in every member of my community, as well as in myself. I look for the goodness in them. Your job, as you just stated, does the opposite. You are looking for the worst in them. The thing that makes one take someone's life. So, you can see I can't help you there. There are some very good people in this congregation and some less so, but I can't imagine any one of them capable of committing murder.'

'Well, as it happens,' Madison said after a pause, 'it has been suggested to me that this might be a hate crime.'

Rabbi Zimmerman stared at the chief inspector with genuine surprise.

'Well – I don't know why, but this just didn't occur to me. It felt so…'

The rabbi hesitated here, and Madison completed the sentence for him.

'It felt so domestic? Is that what you mean?'

'I guess I do,' Rabbi Zimmerman replied. 'It felt so much like… an in-house thing. For someone to be so familiar with our synagogue and the people, and to be able to do it so quickly… Believe me, Chief Inspector, we are very quick – sometimes too quick – to cry antisemitism, but on this occasion it doesn't feel right to me.'

Madison was of the same mind as the rabbi but persisted for a while, following the rule that you have to investigate all avenues.

'Have you had incidents of antisemitism in this synagogue?'

The rabbi smiled, sadly.

'Chief Inspector, this is a synagogue. Of course, we have had incidents of antisemitism. We have been having them for years, although in recent time they have got worse.'

'Actual attacks or just threats?'

'Very violent mail – both email and snail mail. I won't repeat what they say but the office has a record of all such attacks. They can provide you with a sample or more. We are hidden in a not-so-affluent area, so attract less attention than the big Orthodox synagogues. They have a louder presence in the community.'

The two men sat for a while in silence, deep in thought.

'My predecessor – Rabbi Barshevsky – received a nasty email. It was antisemitic but also homophobic. I understand it completely freaked him out. He lived quite close to the synagogue and used to walk here and back. It meant that people in the area knew everything about him. He was petrified – and by all accounts, a bit of a wimp. After that he refused to walk or even drive to the synagogue. He was worried they would recognise his car. He demanded the synagogue provide him with a lift every day – or a taxi if there were no volunteers to chauffer him around.'

Madison did not react. He was not going to judge a civilian terrified of racist or homophobic threats.

These were scary times to be different in any way.

28

Lisa had to admit that Gabbi's – the little café where Jane and Rachel often had their lunch break – was a delightful, charming place.

A strong smell of coffee and croissants met them as they opened the door. Small chatting noise came from three or four tables already occupied. Jane made her way to the back where a table covered in a clean, flowery vinyl table cloth had the menu displayed clearly and a little vase with what looked like fresh flowers.

'What a gorgeous place,' Lisa exclaimed. 'Do they do evening meals?'

Jane almost smiled, in spite of herself.

'Sorry. They close at three p.m. They mostly cater for businesses and shops in the area.'

Lisa checked the menu carefully.

'I think I will go for the croissant sandwich Becky recommended. What will you have?'

Jane was again reticent.

'I will get myself a coffee, thanks,' she said, turning towards the counter.

'Oh, no, you won't,' Lisa said forcefully. 'I practically kidnapped you, so the least I can do is treat you. Croissant sandwich?'

Jane sat down smiling, shyly.

'I guess,' she said. 'And a decaf latte, please.'

Lisa walked to the counter to place her order. She was very pleased she was not in uniform. She could imagine the looks and comments she might have received if she was – and she knew that Jane would have been most uneasy at being seen having lunch with a policewoman.

Having placed her order and paid, Lisa returned to the table and sat down.

'I'm starving,' she said. 'The smells are making my tummy rumble.'

'Officer…' Jane started.

'Please – call me Lisa. I'm not actually an officer, anyhow.'

'Lisa, then,' Jane started again. 'You want to ask me some more questions. Right? Although – I don't know what more I can tell you. I told the chief inspector everything I knew.'

'Not quite everything, Lisa. Was it?'

'What do you mean?'

'You didn't actually tell him what it was Mr Kaufman had on you, personally.'

Jane was quiet for a few minutes, during which the waitress brought over their coffees.

'It has absolutely nothing to do with this,' she said. 'Absolutely nothing.'

'Jane – can I call you Jane?' She waited till Jane shrugged her shoulders, then continued.

'When the police investigate a crime, they amass a lot of information and on average, something like ninety-nine percent of it proves to be irrelevant.'

One of the tutors in the police academy once said that,

and Lisa found it a very useful fact – she never bothered to check its accuracy – when questioning doubting witnesses.

'The thing is,' she continued, 'that at the time of collecting all this information, most of it turning out to be useless, we don't know that it will. It's only at the end of an investigation that we establish what was and what wasn't useful. It is our job to investigate every bit of information until such time that it proves to have been a waste of time.'

'I can promise you,' Jane said, 'that this will be one of those. A complete waste of your time.'

'It may well be,' Lisa said. She fixed her eyes on Jane, making it clear that she was not letting her off the subject.

The waitress came over with their croissants and no one spoke for a while.

'If it comes out – it will be terrible. My life will be… not worth living…'

By this time Lisa had a mouthful of croissant.

'This is even better than I expected,' she managed to say without spitting out the croissant. 'I will have to come back here.'

Jane was not hungry. In fact, she felt sick. Her heart was beating very fast and she wanted to run away from Lisa.

Lisa washed the croissant down with coffee and then looked at Jane.

'If it comes out, Jane,' she said quietly, 'it will not have come from me, or from any of my colleagues. Not unless it has something to do with the case.'

'It doesn't! I know I didn't kill him and that would be the only reason my… story could be of any use to you.'

Even while saying this, Jane knew she was talking nonsense.

'You are forgetting one thing, Jane – Mr Kaufman is gone but Mrs Kaufman is still very much here.'

Jane was confused.

'What are you trying to say?'

'Whatever Mr Kaufman had on you, Mrs Kaufman also has. What makes you think she would not use it?'

Jane looked absolutely terrified.

'I don't know what they know… knew,' she said. 'Cecil… Mr Kaufman never actually said. He hinted at it, without actually saying exactly what he knew. And I never dared ask. And anyhow – what would she have to gain? What could I do for her? God – will this nightmare ever end?'

'I think you would be safer telling us, and we might be able to stop her from ever using it.'

Jane looked down at the croissant sandwich sitting on her plate, untouched.

'I was married for about eight years,' she finally said in a low voice. 'Miserable years… I won't go into details, but we have a daughter… gorgeous girl. She is in high school, doing brilliantly. He was a terrible husband but a really good father. They are very close. He would do anything for her… you know…'

'Daddy's princess syndrome?' Lisa offered, also eyeing Jane's croissant sitting untouched on her plate.

'Something like that.' Jane hesitated. 'The thing is… he is not her father. I mean – biological.'

'I see.'

'No, you don't see. He doesn't know. No one knows… knew… If they found out now, it would ruin everything. She is about to do her GCSEs. It would break her, and him. And the guy – her biological father – he doesn't know. He has a family. It only happened once. We both stopped it from happening again… although he was the love of my life. She is so like him…'

Lisa looked at Jane, all thoughts of another croissant forgotten.

'Don't judge me,' Jane said, looking up at Lisa. 'At the time, I didn't know. It could have been my husband's baby. Only after a few years, as she was getting more and more like… him… I took a DNA test without their knowledge. My husband was definitely not her father. By that time he loved her so much I couldn't tell him.'

Lisa said nothing. She did not want to stop the flow of this confession.

'I never told anyone. Never. Until that night… I never knew you could lose control like that just by having some wine.'

'You think you told them about your daughter?'

'I don't know. That is the maddening thing. I obviously told them something… I will never forgive myself. Don't get me wrong, I would never regret what happened. It gave me my wonderful daughter. I wouldn't be without her for anything, but I know that if she found out, SHE would never forgive me…'

The two women sat for a while in silence.

'You really should get on eating this sandwich,' Lisa said at last.

Jane stood up.

'I can't eat now,' she said. 'I will ask them to pack it for Becky.'

'Thank you, Jane,' Lisa said, standing too. 'I know how difficult this was… I promise you – your secret is safe with us, as long as it doesn't turn out to be a motive.'

'It won't,' Jane said, and walked out of the café.

29

She arrives at the restaurant much too early. She does not want to appear out of breath, all flushed.

She puts her coat carefully over a chair and walks into the ladies' room. There she stands looking at herself in the mirror, trying to see what he will see.

She is aware of fresh wrinkles at the corners of her eyes – laughing marks, she likes to tell herself. Adding character to her face…

She tidies her hair, touches her make-up and stands straighter, like she used to. He never before saw her wearing make-up. Would he notice?

She walks back into the restaurant and stops when she sees him standing by the door, looking around, wondering if he would recognise her.

Then he sees her. Their eyes meet – across a not-so-crowded room – and for a while they don't move. Then she walks slowly towards her table. He follows and joins her at the table. They still look at each other, but nothing is said and there is no touching.

She notices the greying hair. The wrinkles. The thickening of the neck. She likes it. It relaxes her.

She then sits down and he follows her example and sits too. They look at each other to see what twenty years have done to the face they had loved more than anything in the world.

They do not move until the waitress interrupts them, asking what they will have. If she is aware of the 'moment' she is killing, she is not bothered. She has a living to make.

30

'The chief superintendent wants to see me tomorrow morning for a report on our investigation,' Madison said to his team. 'Have any of you got something for me which could get the chief off my back for a few days?'

After an awkward silence, Lisa looked at Madison.

'I am not sure this will get the chief off your back, Jack,' Lisa said hesitantly, 'because it doesn't change much. Maybe only in so much as it gives Jane a really big reason to want Mr Kaufman gone, but she was a suspect anyhow… I did get somewhere with Jane. Miss Barker.'

The three officers looked at Lisa, intrigued.

'She finally told me what was the big secret she suspected Mr Kaufman knew about her. And it's a big one.'

Lisa proceeded to detail the story Jane told her.

'Well done, Lisa,' Madison said when she finished. 'Like you say – it is a big one, but it is not exactly a new angle on the investigation. She is still very much at the top of our suspect list but, we still have no evidence.'

The four officers sat in silence for a while, digesting what they had just heard.

'Josh,' Madison said at last. 'How did you get on with the neighbour? Mr Adams, was it?'

'I didn't, Jack,' Josh replied. 'He wasn't in. I will try again tomorrow.'

'Right,' Madison said, after waiting a while for anyone else to offer some help. 'This is what I want you to do. Get your notes out – everything you have written since we started this investigation – and pass it on to another member of the team. Keep passing reports on until we have all read everyone's notes. There is some paper by the kettle if you wish to take notes while you are reading. You never know what fresh eyes might notice that the writer may have missed. Take your time and read very carefully.'

All four took their notes out – Madison included – and passed them on.

For the next half an hour no one spoke. Everyone was concentrating on reading. All you could hear in the little incident room was the occasional cup returning to the table after a drink was had.

When it was clear that everyone had done with the reading, Madison spoke.

'So? Does anything hit you? It doesn't matter how trivial. Please say whatever thought entered your mind when you were reading. It might be really important.'

After a short hesitation, Lisa was the first to speak.

'I have a problem with Jonson, the caretaker,' she said. 'I don't understand why he was so tetchy about Jack's questioning him… seemed a bit over the top to me.'

'Well,' Brodmann said, 'Jack practically accused him of deliberately keeping from us the fact that there was a direct way from his garden into the synagogue's grounds. Suggesting he had something to hide.'

'I did no such thing,' Jack snapped.

'Well, he certainly got the impression that that was exactly what you were doing,' Brodmann insisted.

‘Even so,’ Lisa continued. ‘I still think he overreacted, which makes me wonder why.’

‘As I told you before,’ Madison said, ‘the rabbi completely vouches for him. He says Jon is as honest as they come.’

‘I’m not sure I would take the rabbi’s word on this,’ Brodmann said quietly.

The room went quiet for a while.

‘Please explain,’ Madison said.

‘How reliable is Rabbi Zimmerman’s word? We know that he deserted a wife in New York and caused his now-wife to desert her husband also. He most likely detested the Kaufmans – with good reason. They were out to destroy him.’

‘Are you suggesting,’ Madison said, realising he was coming across quite aggressively, ‘that the rabbi might have colluded with the caretaker to do away with Mr Kaufman?’

‘I’m not suggesting anything. All I am saying is that we must remember that the rabbi is also a suspect, and therefore, we should treat everything he says with the same scepticism we treat what everyone else is telling us.’

‘Is that not what we are doing?’ Madison asked, hardly hiding his annoyance.

Brodmann had known Madison for years. They had worked together on many cases and, inevitably, occasionally irritated each other. Brodmann could tell that Madison was quite taken with the rabbi and thought he might not be impartial in this matter.

‘I hope it is,’ Brodmann added, making quite sure Madison got the message.

Before Madison could reply to Brodmann, Benson, who had not contributed to the discussion so far, cleared his throat and started speaking in a low voice.

‘Forgive me if I’m speaking out of turn,’ he said. ‘I am new on this team and I’m not sure I should be contributing…’

'Of course, you should be,' Madison said, turning towards the young PC, somewhat relieved. 'I wanted a fresh look and you are probably the freshest pair of eyes in this room. What's on your mind?'

'Well,' Benson started hesitantly. 'I am a little concerned about Becky. The second secretary.'

Madison sat up straighter in his chair.

'Go on,' he said.

'It seems to me that right from the start we were concentrating on Jane – Miss Barker. She came across very nervous. Being so scared of talking to us, she looked guilty. But Becky – Mrs Mosco – she was very different. Very confident and cheerful… and very open. She was happy to talk to us but… I think… maybe we let her off too easily?'

'But Becky has no power at the synagogue. She isn't on the board and she can't influence anyone,' Lisa said.

'I know.' Benson was quick to agree with her. 'That's why I wasn't sure I should mention it. I just thought… she has money problems and she must be in on quite a few things that Miss Barker knows. They are sitting in that room together for hours… sometimes only the two of them. I thought it is inevitable that they talk. It was just a thought…'

Madison smiled at Benson.

'It was a good thought, Josh,' he said. 'You are quite right to point this out. It could mean absolutely nothing, but equally, there might be something there. We should look into it. Would you like to take this on?'

Two assignments in as many days. Josh tried not to show his excitement.

He was quick to assure the chief inspector that he was up for it.

'Good,' Madison said, getting up. 'This was a useful session. Let's keep in mind everything that was said and, if anything else springs to mind, please let us know. Tomorrow morning, I will see the chief, and after that I am finally meeting with the elusive Miss Solomon, the music lady. She is back from her tour but I gave her time to sort herself out and arranged to see her tomorrow. Lisa – fancy coming with me?'

'Sure,' Lisa answered, trying not to sound too excited. She turned to Benson. 'Well done, Josh,' she said softly.

'Yes – well done,' Madison agreed. 'Maybe when we are visiting Miss Solomon you can have a go at Becky? Don't make the same mistake I made with Jonson – be nice. You are young and innocent looking. Try to play on her motherly instincts.'

31

DAY 9

Madison reported to the chief and felt it had gone as well as it could have under the circumstances. Chief superintendents, like every other police officer, knew that investigations took time. Some were quicker to resolve, but others were slower.

The chief was understanding but also anxious to get results as soon as possible. Madison tried to convince him that they were following quite a few leads and hoping for some progress. The chief smiled and remarked that often too many leads take you in too many different directions and obscure the scene. Madison was well aware of that possibility.

As he left headquarters, Madison acknowledged to himself that the chief was on the ball. He felt like he was in a roundabout with too many exits, and he was trying them all but never getting anywhere. He would not confess this to his team, but to himself he had to admit that he was worried. By now, in most investigations, he would begin to have a sense where it was leading and who the more likely suspects were. With this case, it seemed that with every step forwards he was walking two backwards.

Back in his car, Madison took his phone out and made a swift call.

'Lisa,' he spoke into the phone, 'I'm running a little late. Can you meet me at the house? … You have the address? … Good. See you there. I should be no longer than fifteen minutes.'

Madison started the car and pulled out of the car park. He was curious about Miki Solomon. As motives go, she had a good one. Apparently, although she resigned she was pushed into it by Mr Kaufman. Was that enough to satisfy her sense of revenge?

Madison did not often lose his temper while questioning suspects or witnesses, and he was cross with himself for losing it with Mr Jonson. He was not going to make that mistake again with Miss Solomon, whatever the provocation.

32

Madison pulled up outside the house just as Lisa got off her moped and was taking her helmet off.

'If I was your father,' Madison said as he walked nearer to Lisa, 'I would be worried about you riding this machine.'

'Well, you are not my father, gov.' She remembered that in public – although right now no one could hear them – Madison preferred to be addressed as gov. She also wished he would not think of her in a 'fatherly' way. 'And my father is much more worried about me being in this job,' she snapped, 'than about my chosen form of transport. Mind you – if the job paid better, I might be able to afford a car.'

Madison smiled. He would've liked to be able to tell her father his daughter was safe in his care, but he knew he could not make such promises. Madison worried about the young officers joining the force and wished he could keep them safe.

'So – let's do it,' he said, starting to walk towards the house.

It was a small, semidetached bungalow. The front garden had been tarmacked and offered two parking spaces. A small, white Citroën – presumably Miss Solomon's – was occupying one space.

The bungalow seemed well looked after – windows recently painted. Nothing on the outside could give a hint as to the character of the owner.

Madison rang the doorbell and smiled at Lisa coming up behind him.

It took a couple of minutes for the door to open, and the two policemen got their first glimpse of Miki Solomon.

They knew Miki to be in her forties, but she could have been any age between thirty and fifty. She had an air of confidence of someone well aware of the impression they leave on people. A captivating smile exaggerated the high cheekbones, above which shone green eyes that were carefully studying the two officers on her doorstep. Her face was crowned with a mass of curls that mischievously danced between the streaks of colour – brown, gold and copper. She was wearing black, tight leggings and a loose shirt over it.

Madison had his warrant card ready in his hand but, for the moment, stood staring at her, saying nothing.

Lisa waited for her boss to say something, glanced at him, and then took the initiative.

'Miss Solomon?' she said, holding up her warrant card.

'I guess so, yes,' Miss Solomon answered with a cheeky smile on her face, 'although I would prefer Miki.'

To Lisa's relief, Madison found his voice again.

'DCI Jack Madison and PC Lisa Thompson,' he said, also holding up his warrant card for Miss Solomon to see.

'Please come in,' Miki said, holding the door wide open for them to walk through. 'First door on your left,' she said as she closed the front door after them.

The two officers walked into the living room.

'Can I get you a drink? Coffee? Tea? Something stronger?'

Madison, who had been studying Miss Solomon intently, said suddenly, 'Have we met before, Miss Solomon?'

Lisa was on the point of saying yes, please, to a cup of coffee. She looked at her boss, perplexed.

Miss Solomon was quiet for a moment, trying to decide whether to react to the fact that the chief inspector used Miss Solomon, in spite of the fact that she asked to be called Miki.

She returned his look, checking Madison up and down provocatively.

'I don't think so, DCI Jack Madison,' she said at last, with a glint in her eye. 'I think I would have remembered…'

Madison was not easily embarrassed, but he felt strangely uncomfortable.

'I would love a cup of coffee,' Lisa said hurriedly, trying to lighten the mood although, for the life of her, she did not understand what caused the atmosphere in the first place.

Miss Solomon left the room without repeating the offer to Madison.

In her absence, the two officers did what came naturally to well-trained police officers – they took the opportunity to study the room they were in.

It was certainly different. There were musical instruments hanging on the wall – violins, old string instruments, some strange African percussion instruments. In the corner of the room stood a small grand piano. There were bits of music strewn all over the piano – some on the music stand and some over the body of the piano. Pictures on the wall seemed to have old music manuscripts as well as photos of Miss Solomon, sometimes playing the piano and sometimes playing the violin as part of an ensemble.

The room was alive with music.

'I apologise for the mess,' Miss Solomon said as she walked in carrying two mugs of coffee. 'I am trying to organise my music. It was a crazy tour. Up to two concerts a day. Sugar?'

Lisa declined and Miss Solomon put her cup on the little coffee table. She then took the second cup of coffee and settled with it in one of the armchairs.

'You were on tour?' Madison asked. 'Where to?'

'Europe. France, Germany and Holland.'

'With an orchestra?'

'No. Nothing grand like that. Just a piano trio.'

Lisa was struggling with her coffee in one hand and a notebook in the other. She was beginning to regret having asked for coffee she didn't need.

'Chief Inspector,' Miss Solomon said, 'I could give you the full itinerary of our European tour but I have a feeling this is not what you really want to know.'

Madison gave her one of his stern looks. She was either as innocent as the day she was born, or a very shrewd, calculating killer.

'I understand you visited the synagogue on your way to the airport?' he started.

'That's right. I left some music in the choir cupboard and I wanted to take it on tour with me. I was meeting with a choir master in Holland and wanted to show him the music.'

'The choir cupboard is up in the balcony?'

Miss Solomon put down her cup and looked at Madison.

'That's correct. I guess that makes me a suspect?'

'Everyone who was at the synagogue that day is a suspect, Miss Solomon. You are not singled out.'

'Well – for what it's worth – I ran in, up the stairs, into the cupboard, collected the music and ran out.'

'Did you see anyone during all this running?'

'I had a word with the secretaries after they let me in, but other than that I saw no one.'

Madison reacted with one of his well-known silences. These often got more results than aggressive questioning.

Miss Solomon returned his look and replied with a silence all of her own.

When it was clear to Madison that she was not going to break the silence, he did.

'Did you hear about Mr Kaufman's… er… fall when you were on tour?'

'Yes, I did. A few members of the choir emailed me.'

'How did you react when you heard the news?'

'How do you think? I was shocked.'

'But not heartbroken?'

Miss Solomon gave Madison a cold look.

'If you want to ask me how I felt about Mr Kaufman, why don't you just ask?'

'I'm sorry. You are right. How did you feel about Mr Kaufman?'

'He was a detestable human being. I know you are not supposed to say that about the departed but that is the truth. I will not miss him but I can assure you I did not kill him.'

'What caused you to say he was a detestable man?'

Without looking away from the chief inspector, Miss Solomon said, 'You know. Don't you?'

There was silence in the room.

'I'm not sure I know what you think I know, Miss Solomon.'

'I am sure I was not the only person he tried to blackmail,' she said at last.

'So, he tried to blackmail you. Did he succeed?'

'He did not.'

'Can you tell me more about it?'

'Not before I know what you already know on the matter.'

'What makes you think I know…'

'You have been talking to people for a week while I was away. Enough time for people to gossip.'

'Miss Solomon, I don't normally talk about other… witnesses… but I feel I must tell you. You are wrong there. The person you are referring to did not "gossip" to anyone – and if they talked to us, it was their duty. This is a murder investigation.'

Miss Solomon held the chief inspector's gaze, trying to understand what he had just said.

Madison went on.

'What was it that Mr Kaufman knew about you?'

'Why would that be of any interest to you?'

'I don't know. Yet. When we put all the information together, we will find out what is of interest and what is not.'

'Well – you can take my word, Chief Inspector. It is of no interest to you and will not help you find whoever killed Cecil… Mr Kaufman.'

'I'm sorry, Miss Solomon, but it is up to me to decide whether this information will be helpful or not.'

Madison noticed that Miss Solomon glanced at Lisa before looking back at him.

'I can assure you, Miss Solomon, that no one will hear about it from us – unless, of course, it becomes evidence in a trial.'

'It will not, Chief Inspector. It is… something from my very far past.'

Miss Solomon put her cup down and took a moment to organise her thoughts.

'It was a long time ago… It happened in Israel and it stayed in Israel. It was not part of my life here and I never told anyone about it. I think I might have dropped a hint when I met with Jane… I'm not sure I did, but the fact that Cecil seemed to have known about it would suggest she told him. I never expected her to… anyhow, it was nothing really. Even had she told him, he would have no idea what it was about because she also did not know…'

Madison fixed his eyes on her, waiting for her to continue. When, again, this technique seemed to fail, he was forced to ask, 'Mr Kaufman threatened you?'

'He tried to,' Miss Solomon said with contempt. 'He hinted at something but it was obvious to me that he really knew nothing. He tried to convince me that he knew more than he did, so it was very easy to laugh it off. I told him to go ahead and tell everyone what he knew… which was basically nothing… and unless you put me on trial and force me to talk about it, this is all I am prepared to say on the matter.'

The tone of her voice assured Madison that there was no point pressuring her any further.

'Let's hope, Miss Solomon, that there will not be a need to do that,' Madison said, standing up.

Lisa hurriedly closed her notebook and stood up next to Madison.

At the door, with Lisa already on her way to her moped, Madison turned to Miss Solomon and said quietly, 'I think you should have a word with Miss Barker. It's not what you think it is…'

And with that, he turned and walked to his car.

33

Benson parked his car in the synagogue's car park and walked around the block on his way to Mr Adams's house. Of the two jobs the chief inspector had allocated to him, this was the easier one. He was not looking forward to interviewing Becky. Doing this in the office would be really awkward with Jane listening in, and he didn't feel he had the authority to ask her to come into their incident room. He definitely did not feel he had it in him to ask her to have coffee with him at the little café. Women knew how to do these things.

So, he chose the easier job and made his way to Mr Adams's house for the second time.

A car was parked on the drive. That was a good sign. A little Smart car. Many older people seemed to choose this car for their second car to run around town in, but Benson didn't think Mr Adams's lifestyle stretched to two cars. There was no garage and it was a safe bet that this little car was the only set of wheels Mr Adams owned.

Mr Jonson and Mr Adams occupied the two middle houses in a row of four terraces. Mr Adams's seemed more cared for. Benson guessed that, as the saying went, the shoemaker's children always go barefoot – Jonson spent hours doing jobs in the synagogue and clearly had no time, or inclination, to work on his own house.

Whereas Mr Adams had flower baskets hanging in the front, and a big, blue hydrangea blossoming happily under his front window. Jonson's front garden although tidy, had no flowers at all.

Benson walked to the front door and pressed the doorbell.

It did not take long for the door to be opened by Mr Adams.

Benson was faced by a large man – how he ever got into the Smart car was a mystery – with what seemed to be a permanent smile on his round face.

'And what can I be doing for you, young man?' Mr Adams almost sang this greeting in a big, bass voice.

'Mr Adams?' Benson asked while presenting his warrant card.

'Ah – police!' Benson was further pleased to see that the smile was still there. 'Bad business that!' Mr Adams said and motioned Benson to come in. 'Jon said you might be talking to me, although I can't imagine what I can tell you. Come in, come in. I'm afraid the wife has a meeting in the living room. I hope you don't mind coming in the kitchen with me.'

Benson followed Mr Adams into the kitchen.

In his short time with the police, Benson had already been in worse places than this small, warm kitchen that smelled of coffee and baking. It reminded him of his grandmother's kitchen.

'Kitchen,' he said. 'My favourite room of the house.'

'Tea or coffee?'

'Tea, please.' Unless he was drinking the coffee he made himself, Benson always opted for tea. Less insulting to his taste buds.

'So,' Mr Adams said over the noise of the electric kettle. 'How can I be helping you? I have little to do with the synagogue. I'm good friends with Jon. Help him sometimes with his gardening – he is too busy, and quite honestly, not that way inclined … but that's as far as it goes.'

That explains it, Benson said to himself. Jonson's garden was not eye catching in any way, but remarkably tidy.

'I understand you carry a spare set of keys for Mr Jonson's house?'

'Guilty!' Mr Adams said, putting both his hands up and laughing too much at his own joke. Seeing that it fell rather flat, he got back to preparing the tea. 'Yes, I do have the keys to his house but this is really just in case he locks himself out or, once, his daughter arrived and had left her keys at home.'

'And apart from Mr Jonson or his daughter, you never gave the keys to anyone else?'

'Never!' Mr Adams said as he brought the cups to the kitchen counter, where they settled themselves on the high stools. 'Who would I give it to? No one ever comes to visit Jon – not when he is out.'

Benson took a few sips of his tea before saying, 'Can I go out into your garden, Mr Adams?'

'Into the garden? Why? What for?'

'No special reason. I just… would like to take a look.'

Mr Adams pulled a face but picked up his cup and walked to the kitchen door.

Benson followed him. The garden was quite small and well hidden from prying eyes. The rear of the garden, backing onto the synagogue's grounds, had a really high border. Benson walked closer and inspected it.

'You don't have a gate opening into the synagogue's grounds, do you?' he asked.

'We don't, no. When we first moved in here, before the synagogue was built, we had some kind of a social club over there. All sorts were coming and going. We didn't want any of them peeping over into our garden, so we planted this tall border.'

Benson had seen enough.

'Thank you very much, Mr Adams. That will be all,' he said as he walked back into the kitchen and put his cup – half drunk – in the sink.

Benson doubted very much that the solution to their investigation lay in Mr Adams's garden.

34

The waitress takes their order – one they will not consume – and leaves.

Slowly, he moves his hand along the table until it reaches hers.

A current passes through their bodies.

It is still there. As it had been then. But this time they will just hold hands. They will talk – as soon as they catch their breath – and they will hold hands and lock eyes until they part, probably forever. The likelihood of ever again being in the same country, same town, same time is so unrealistic that they will hold each other's hands till the last minute.

Now that their love is no longer forbidden, they can allow it to fly away and release them.

35

DAY 10

'I met with Becky Mosco and also with Mr Adams yesterday.' Benson started giving his report to the team, assembled in the tiny incident room. 'Mr Kaufman has a set of spare keys to Jonson's house but I honestly don't think there is more to this. He showed me his garden – there is no way through his very tall hedge into the synagogue's grounds. He once gave the keys to Mr Jonson's daughter when she left her own keys at home. In fact, he took a while remembering where he kept the spare key, as he had not used it for a very long time. I really don't think he has any part in this business.'

'You are probably right, Josh,' Madison said. 'We will keep him on the back burner for now, but it's good you covered that. What about Becky Mosco?'

'Well – if she is hiding anything, I haven't discovered it, Jack,' Benson admitted. 'I managed to talk to her as she was leaving to go home so she was on her own. She had no problem admitting that money was tight. Her husband is not well and had to retire early and her salary doesn't go a long way. She loves her job… didn't like Mr Kaufman but, from what I could tell, he didn't bother her personally. Of course, she might be a very cool actress and might have told me lies. I didn't want to come out and ask point blank if he was blackmailing her… you know… if he wasn't, I didn't want to suggest the idea to her.'

'You did well,' Madison said. 'Anyone else?'

'I took Jane – Miss Barker – out for lunch in this delicious little café,' Lisa said. 'It's all in my notes here. I must tell you – this café is a real find. You should go in there while we are still on this case. The smell of the place is to die for and what with the coffee and fantastic croissants—'

'Lisa!' Madison interrupted. 'Miss Barker?'

'Sorry, I get distracted easily by good food. Yes, Miss Barker. She did tell me – reluctantly – what it was all about… and Jack, I really hope we can keep it just between us. If it comes out it will ruin her life and her daughter's also. I honestly find it hard to believe that she had anything to do with the murder. She wouldn't hurt a fly. At least that's my feeling about her. And anyhow, Mrs Kaufman knew all about it too, so what did she have to gain by killing only Mr Kaufman? I just don't see it, Jack.'

'Yet another suspect bites the dust!' Madison declared in mock despair. 'Are any of you ever going to say, I think this one did it? Because, mates, we are paid to find a guilty person, not to find everyone innocent!'

The rest of the team smiled in sympathy. So far, they had declared between them three unlikely suspects – Jon, Becky and the neighbour. And Madison's gut feeling about the rabbi made a fourth.

'Well,' Josh started hesitantly.

'Come on, Josh,' Madison said. 'If you have something to say, say it.'

'It's only… Becky mentioned someone that we have not heard about before.'

Everyone turned their eyes on Benson.

'Someone connected to the murder?' Madison pressed Benson.

'That's just it. I don't know. But it's someone who had it in for Miss Solomon and who worked together with Mr Kaufman to push her out.'

Madison was amazed.

'How come we didn't hear about this before?'

'She was not at the synagogue on that day. At that stage we were only looking at people who were at the synagogue that morning.'

Madison knew that was a mistake and he blamed himself for it – although not very publicly.

'Let's hear it then, Josh.'

Benson stood up, then felt really stupid, behaving like he was still at school, and sat down again.

'Molly,' he said. 'Molly Rubin.'

'Who is she?' Madison asked.

'She is a member of the synagogue and recently has become a member of the board. Becky says she had a strange love-hate relationship with Miss Solomon.'

Benson related to the group the little information Becky gave him on Molly Rubin.

'Probably yet another very innocent suspect,' Madison muttered, 'but I will check her out. I can't get rid of the feeling that it has something to do with Mr Jonson's house and the back gate… it just keeps nagging at me…'

36

Mrs Kaufman made it her business to always see what was happening outside her house. Her armchair was situated in such a way that she could always see outside her window, as well as watch the TV that was stationed above a small chest of drawers.

'You never know who might be loitering outside the door,' she used to say to Mr Kaufman. 'I want to have a prior warning if someone is watching the house. This is always a sign they are planning a break-in.'

Mr Kaufman's armchair was facing her, enabling him to see the TV but not quite so easily the outside.

Mrs Kaufman did not like change, and so she preferred her husband's chair to still be there, in the same position, although he was never going to be sitting in it again. Sometimes she would catch herself talking to him, as if he was still there. She assured herself that this was normal and that, with time, the habit would disappear.

'Oh, no!' she exclaimed to the empty chair. 'It's that dreadful policeman again.' She watched Madison getting out of his car. Someone else was getting out of the passenger's side of the car. She looked carefully. 'Oh – it's Sergeant Brodmann with him. Why couldn't he just come on his own? I guess the other one gives the orders.'

Mrs Kaufman switched off the television and stood up. She had been hoping that Sergeant Brodmann would come to visit her again, but the chief inspector was bound to ruin the visit.

She stood in the living room, waiting for the doorbell to ring. When it did, she made her way to the door slowly.

'Mrs Kaufman,' Madison said when she finally opened the door. 'Can we come in?'

'Sergeant Brodmann!' Mrs Kaufman said in a welcoming voice, completely ignoring the chief inspector. 'Come in. Please.'

Madison moved to let the sergeant walk in first, but followed him quickly, fearing the door would be shut in his face.

Mrs Kaufman led them into the living room, and motioned Brodmann to sit in her deceased husband's chair. She herself sat back in her own chair and the chief inspector was left to choose a seat on the sofa, which was some way away from the armchairs.

Madison was not put off by this treatment. He had already guessed that there would be no lemon drizzle, so there was nothing to lose by a direct approach.

'Mrs Kaufman,' he started, 'we need to ask you a few questions.'

Mrs Kaufman turned to look at Madison, as if just noticing he was there.

'Am I a suspect, Chief Inspector?' she asked, confrontationally.

'Mrs Kaufman, I am sure you want to help us find your husband's killer. Don't you?'

'I don't know how I can help. I have spoken to you before and you don't seem to have got anywhere in your investigation.'

She pronounced the word 'investigation' with contempt.

'Mrs Kaufman,' Madison continued, dropping all attempt at 'kid gloving' her. 'I understand that you and your husband knew things… about people…'

'Knew things?' Mrs Kaufman sat up in her chair. 'What do you mean?'

'I think you know what I mean,' Madison persisted.

Mrs Kaufman glanced at Brodmann, as if demanding that he interfere. Brodmann looked away.

'I am simply trying to find out who had a motive to do away with your husband, Mrs Kaufman. And I understand that you both gathered information about people in the congregation and that Mr Kaufman used this information to get a position on the board. I need to know who these people were.'

If Madison hoped Mrs Kaufman would be bothered by these revelations, he was going to be disappointed. Far from looking frightened, she seemed angry.

'Why are you asking me?' she demanded. 'It is obvious that you have spoken to people who said these vicious things about us. Do you really expect me to corroborate these allegations?'

She looked directly at Brodmann, expecting him to rush to her defence. Brodmann felt he had to say something.

'Mrs Kaufman,' he started meekly, 'the chief inspector is not making any accusations. He is simply trying to—'

'Mrs Kaufman,' Madison interrupted his sergeant. 'We think your husband was murdered by one of these people he was… well, putting pressure on. Someone who wanted to stop him from passing on personal information. Now, seeing that you obviously are in possession of vital information, it is possible that your life is also in danger. Do you understand?'

'I understand very well! You come here, uninvited, when I am still mourning my husband. You sit in my house, saying the most vile things about my husband and myself, and you expect me to help you?'

Mrs Kaufman stood up.

'Please leave my house this minute. And the next time you want to talk to me, please announce yourself in advance and I will make sure to have my solicitor with me.'

The two men stood up.

'I'm really sorry, Mrs Kaufman,' Brodmann murmured. 'We didn't mean to…'

'I am very disappointed in you, Sergeant. I thought you were a better man. You know where the door is.'

At the door, Madison turned to face Mrs Kaufman.

'We will talk again, Mrs Kaufman,' Madison said. 'If not here then at the station, but we will talk again.'

And with that the two officers walked out of the house.

'I'm really sorry, Mrs Kaufman…' Madison mimicked the sergeant, when they were at a safe hearing distance from the house.

'Well, you did go at her like a bull in a china shop.'

'A bull maybe – but a china shop?'

Madison unlocked the car and the two got in. He started the car and moved out of sight of the house. He then relaxed and started laughing. When Madison laughed it was impossible not to laugh with him. He had a deep, roaring laughter, like a big rock bouncing down a mountain, gathering momentum as it rolled faster and faster.

Brodmann tried to resist but failed, and in a couple of minutes he was also roaring with laughter.

'What's… what's so funny?' he asked stupidly, while laughing louder and louder.

'If you don't know what's funny' – Madison exploded with hilarity – 'why are you laughing?'

That only made the two men laugh even more. Madison stopped the car and wiped away tears of laughter.

'China shop,' Madison repeated. 'Mrs Kaufman… china shop…'

The two laughed uncontrollably.

After a while, the laughter started dying down. They looked at each other and Brodmann commented, 'Not really that funny, was it?'

Which only started them laughing some more.

Eventually, Madison felt confident enough to drive and started the car.

'I needed that,' he said, checking his mirror before moving out.

'OK, Dave,' Madison said after a while. 'I will not ask you to visit this particular china shop again.'

Brodman appreciated that but did not reply.

The two officers had worked together many years and quite often disagreed, but never before had Brodmann's Jewishness come between them while investigating a crime.

Neither of them liked this change in their relationship.

37

Madison dropped Brodmann at the synagogue to write up his notes and drove on. He just needed time on his own.

Lisa had recommended the little café and Madison thought this would be a good time to try it. Away from everyone, so he could concentrate and think. He always found it easier to concentrate when on his own.

He walked into the café and, rather than the quiet little corner café he was expecting, the place was packed. Lisa was right about the smell. It was alcohol-free intoxication.

He thought, *Coffee and one of these croissant sandwiches and out to the car*. He could drink and eat in peace.

The girl at the till suggested he find a seat while they prepared his order.

Madison looked around. Every table was taken. And then, his eyes locked on Miki Solomon sitting in the corner on her own.

Their eyes met briefly. Miki glanced around the room and saw there were no empty seats. She looked up at him and, after a slight hesitation, pointed to the empty seat across her table.

Madison walked slowly to her table.

'I'm not really staying,' he said. 'Just waiting for my order.'

'Well, you can sit down while you are waiting, Chief Inspector,' she said, sounding amused.

Madison pulled the chair out and sat down.

Miki Solomon noticed that Madison briefly looked at the empty cup on his side of the table.

'That was Jane's cup,' she said. 'She had to get back to work. I… I took your advice,' she said sheepishly. 'Thank you.'

'That's good,' Madison said.

An awkward silence fell between them.

'What a bastard that man was!' Miki broke the silence and Madison was a little taken back. 'There I go again speaking ill of the dead, but I've always wondered about that. Hitler is dead and we freely speak ill of him and other evil people. Dying is not a free ticket to sainthood.'

A hint of a smile appeared on Madison's face and disappeared so quickly she doubted he had actually smiled.

'He was not a good man,' he said, and thanked the waitress for his coffee and croissant that just arrived.

'Not a good man?' she asked. 'I can't believe that at the time Jane needed me most, I wasn't there for her. He put her through absolute hell. No – he wasn't a very good man! Understatement.'

Madison wondered if, as was his original intention, he should bid Miki goodbye and walk out to his car. But he stayed sitting. He sampled the coffee and had to agree it was very fine. He looked at her for a little while, curiously.

Miki was wearing a red jacket with brass buttons which gave her something of a military image, contrasting with her hair falling freely in waves, through which an occasional glimpse at her long red earrings, matching her jacket, completed the picture.

Madison noticed he had been staring at her, causing an awkwardness between them.

‘I have not worked with musicians before,’ he said, breaking the silence. ‘I am wondering if it wasn’t very stifling working in a synagogue with all its dos and don’ts.’

‘You would be surprised,’ Miki replied, ‘to realise that music is full of dos and don’ts and rules and what you can and can’t do.’

Madison took a minute to think.

‘I’m sure you are right, but I was thinking more on a human level. I always believed musicians to be free… cosmopolitan… not restricted so much by the society rules.’

It was Miki’s turn to pause.

‘To some extent you are right. Although you can find musicians that are every bit as stuffy and restricted as any synagogue goer… the best musicians probably fit your idea of us. They can afford to be – and I don’t only talk of money. When you are a genius, people make allowances.’

She stopped again and Madison watched her as she organised her thoughts before speaking them.

‘But there are things that surprised me working at the synagogue. Some of the musicians I studied with and later worked with were – are – incredibly brilliant. You can tell the special ones almost from the beginning. I think that when you are so talented and music is so much part of you, you just can’t tolerate mediocrity. You expect the highest performance from yourself as well as from others. Hearing or playing with mediocre musicians is physical torture, which is why they would often “misbehave” when making music with others. It is generally considered having a big ego. When I started working at the synagogue, I soon found out that even very mediocre people with very little talent can have big egos… that talent just didn’t have a role, and you didn’t need to be special to reach the top. You could have the tantrums and expect the respect you did not earn. That just by clawing your way to the top of however small an institution you would be rewarded with power and accolades… sorry. I'm afraid I'm boring you.'

'On the contrary,' Madison protested. 'I find this fascinating.'

'As a policeman?'

'As a man… a person. I am wondering – which group would you include yourself in? The brilliant ones who are allowed to "misbehave"?'

'I'm afraid not,' Miki replied. 'I'm good but not that good. But I still expect a lot of myself and others, and I am probably not nice to be around when I don't get it.'

Madison had a bite of the croissant and, again, had to admit that Lisa was right. It was delicious.

He drank down the coffee and looked up to find Miki observing him with interest.

'What is it?' he enquired.

'You know a lot about me,' she said at last. 'I know nothing about you.'

'That's the way it is supposed to work,' Madison said.

'Ah, well,' Miki said, and started gathering her things.

'What exactly do you want to know about me?' Madison asked, surprising himself. He did not want her to leave.

'Something… anything.' She relaxed her hold on her bag and remained sitting. 'Are you married?'

That took Madison by surprise.

'I was,' he answered at last.

'I see… divorced?'

A cloud appeared in his eyes and disappeared instantly, but she noticed it.

'I'm sorry… it's none of my business.'

'She died,' he answered at last.

'I'm so sorry,' she said quickly. 'I never learn.'

'Anything else you want to know?' Madison asked. The cloud disappeared and he looked somewhat amused.

Miki was not amused. She looked down at the table and then up at him.

'How much did Jane tell you about… me?'

'Not much. She didn't seem to know very much…'

'No. I told her very little… which is why I knew Cecil had nothing on me.'

'She referred to your "secret" as your "forbidden love".'

Miki was obviously very uncomfortable.

'I wish I'd never mentioned it… I don't usually.'

Madison allowed the silence to live for a while.

'In what way was it forbidden?' he asked at last.

She turned and looked at him with resentment.

'You can't help it, can you?' she said.

'Can't help what?' he asked.

'Being a policeman.'

'I didn't ask as a policeman,' Madison said quietly.

Miki studied his face, as if trying to decide if he meant what he said.

'Calling it that got me in trouble.'

'How?'

'The word "forbidden" can be interpreted in different ways. One member of the synagogue who happened to hear it clearly got the wrong idea.'

'Molly Rubin?' Madison suggested.

Miki looked at him in astonishment.

'How did you know that?'

'I am a police officer,' Madison said. 'People talk to me.'

'You didn't talk to Molly. Did you?'

'Not yet,' he answered. 'I have to warn you that from this moment I'm probably back in uniform – so to speak.'

'I will need another cup of coffee if we're going into this business.'

She stood up but Madison stopped her.

'Let me get this one, please. This is the least I can do, having infringed on your privacy.'

She watched him at the counter, ordering her coffee. His ease with the staff, the way they responded to him immediately, not keeping him waiting as was their habit. Even out of uniform he had an air of authority about him. Or was it his good looks?

As Madison glanced in her direction, he caught her looking at him.

'Sugar?' he mouthed without sound.

She mouthed back, 'No.'

She should have said she would like a sweetener. Why on earth could she not tell him that? She was annoyed with herself.

'Thanks.' She welcomed the hot drink and put her hands around the cup. It was a habit since childhood. It gave her comfort.

Madison offered her two sweetener sachets.

She looked at him in amazement.

'How…?'

Madison did not smile but he looked at her with evident glee.

'I would like to pretend that it was the result of my superior detecting skills,' Madison admitted, mischievously, 'but the girl on the counter told me you take sweeteners.'

Miki was furious with herself. Why couldn't she just have told him herself? Why did she care if he knew she was trying to lose a few pounds?

'You were talking about Molly Rubin,' Madison said, and for once, Miki was relieved to change the subject.

'I have known Molly since she was a child,' she started. 'I taught her the piano. She was quite talented but no Mozart – sorry, that was quite nasty. How many people are Mozarts? Anyhow, she was quite attached to me. I didn't think too much about it as – well, children get attached to teachers, don't they?'

I can see why they would get attached to you, Madison thought, but did not say.

'Well,' she continued, 'she stopped playing the piano but started coming to the synagogue choir when I took it over. Again, I didn't think much about it but she became more needy. More clingy. She wanted to come for singing lessons; wanted my advice on things; always looked for reasons to stay and talk after rehearsals. I didn't worry too much about it – with hindsight I probably should have… Anyhow, she is a clever girl but a non-achiever with a very poor social life. She is not very attractive but what I found disconcerting was the look in her eyes… Throughout rehearsals she would be watching me with this greedy look in her eyes, as if she wanted something from me. When she joined the synagogue's board she became drunk on power. Like I said before – everyone is looking for a small enough pool. The smaller the pool the bigger they feel… She befriended Cecil, Mr Kaufman, as he was attempting to become the chair. I didn't realise it then but since learning what Cecil had discovered about my past, I put two and two together. I am sure he told her about my – I wish I hadn't referred to it with this stupid name. This was at the same time that she came out as gay, and looking back on it, I am fairly sure that she interpreted the "forbidden love" as a gay love. The reason I think this is because her attachment to me became almost obsessive at this point. I didn't deal with it very well. I started avoiding her. Being rejected by a straight woman is almost tolerable… but being rejected by one she thought of as gay, that was too much. At this point she completely changed, became hostile, argumentative, misbehaved in rehearsals. And then I found out that she and Cecil had cooked up a complaint against me. No matter how good you are at what you do – in fact, the better you are, the more there will be people trying to knock you down. There have been complaints about me in the past but previous chairs knew how to deal with them. To be honest, I just couldn't be bothered with it. So, I resigned.'

Madison listened intently. He didn't speak until he was sure she had finished.

'You must have resented the two of them very much,' he said finally. 'Between them they brought about the culmination of your work at the synagogue?'

Miki looked straight at Madison. Her eyes betrayed her anger.

'You did warn me you were back in uniform,' she said, and gathered her things. 'You are right. If you are looking for motives – I certainly had one. Thank you for the coffee.'

Without another word, she walked away from him and out of the café.

38

DAY 11

Madison arrived at the dental practice without notifying anyone at the practice of his visit in advance. Occasionally he liked to surprise a witness.

'How can I help you?' a voice greeted him as he approached reception.

'I am looking for a Molly Rubin,' Madison replied, flashing his warrant card.

He had no doubt that the person he was looking at was Molly. She fitted the descriptions he had heard from a few people.

Molly was tall, but gave the impression of being small because of her poor posture. Miki had described her eyes as 'greedy', which at the time puzzled him, but Madison could see what Miki meant. She had the look of a person who wanted too much and got very little.

If she had been a friend, Madison would have told her to do something with her hair – but as she was not, he could only wonder what made some people spend a lot of money on haircuts that only emphasised their worst features. Molly had a podgy, protruding nose, made all the more obvious by a short, spiky haircut on one side and complete baldness on the other. The lack of hair also emphasised a multitude of skin problems.

There was now a new look in her eyes which Miki possibly never encountered – fear.

'What is it you want?' she spat out, trying to sound aggressive but betraying her apprehension.

'Detective Chief Inspector Madison,' he replied.

'Are you Molly Rubin?'

'What if I am?' she answered, defiantly. 'Have I driven through a red light or something?'

'I don't know,' Madison answered. 'Have you?'

He stood there looking at her, sensing her defiance melting at the strength of his stare.

'If it's about the… murder at the synagogue,' she finally relented, 'I know nothing about it.'

As if he hadn't heard this, Madison continued.

'Is there anywhere we can talk, Miss Rubin?'

'I can't… you can see I'm working,' she mumbled.

'Don't you get a break?' Madison asked, pointedly turning his eyes to the waiting room, which was empty.

'I do, but not…'

Molly glanced at the office window, through which Madison could clearly see two women sitting at their desks and looking at them, intrigued.

One of the women stood up and walked out of the office towards them.

'Is there a problem, Molly?' She might have been talking to Molly but her eyes were fixed on Madison. From her tone of authority, she was clearly in charge.

Madison produced his card.

'DCI Madison,' he said, loud enough to be heard in the office also.

‘Police?’ she asked. ‘How can we help?’

‘It is Molly here that I need to talk to,’ Madison replied, aware that he was making it more awkward for Molly but quite happy to do so. He wanted Molly out of her comfort zone by the time the questioning started.

‘Molly?’ the woman, obviously Molly’s boss, looked at Molly disapprovingly. ‘What could you possibly be wanting with Molly?’

‘It’s nothing to do with me,’ Molly said hurriedly. ‘It’s the synagogue—’

‘Could Molly be excused for a few minutes, Miss…?’ Madison left the ‘Miss’ hanging in the air.

‘Mrs,’ the woman replied. ‘Mrs Davidson. Molly,’ she said, turning to Molly with obvious displeasure, ‘you can take your lunch break early. I will man the desk till your return. You can take the… inspector to the staff room.’

Molly was almost on the verge of tears. She left the reception desk and walked away, with Madison following her.

As they entered the staff room, she turned to him, clearly upset.

‘You are going to lose me my job!’ she said, trying to hold back her tears.

‘I am really sorry about that, Miss Rubin,’ Madison said. ‘I hope your boss will understand. This is a murder case.’

‘It’s nothing to do with me,’ Molly protested. ‘I know absolutely nothing about it. I’m going back to the desk. I can’t lose my job over this nonsense.’

She turned and made for the door. Madison’s calm and steady voice stopped her.

‘If you’d rather, Miss Rubin, I will take you in and we can continue this at the police station.’

Molly turned around and looked at Madison with a look of resentment but also fear.

'Please sit down,' Madison said, pulling a chair for himself and sitting down.

Reluctantly, Molly did the same. For a while, they stared at each other, till Molly lowered her eyes.

'I am a little surprised,' Madison said, 'at your negative attitude. Everyone else I interviewed seemed keen to help.'

'Well – they might know something. I don't. I can't help you.'

Madison held back for a while, never taking his eyes off her, which made her more nervous.

'You knew Mr Kaufman well, didn't you?'

'I knew him,' she snapped. 'Everyone knew him.'

'But you were quite close to him, were you not?'

'Who said that? Who told you I was close to him? I bet I know.'

'You know who told me you were close to Mr Kaufman?'

'I can imagine.'

Madison gave her time to expand on it, but she said nothing.

'Actually, quite a few people told me that. Why do you mind it so much?'

'Because people don't know what they are talking about,' Molly said.

'So, they are wrong when they say you and Mr Kaufman were very close?' Madison stressed the point.

'Dead wrong. I hated him!'

Madison jumped on this, giving her not a minute to pull back.

'Enough to kill him?' he asked.

Molly froze.

Through gritted teeth, and struggling to find her voice, Molly said, 'I didn't kill him.'

In the silence that followed, Madison kept staring at Molly, watching her wriggling in her chair and moving her eyes around the room, avoiding his.

'I wasn't even there,' she protested. 'I thought you were only interested in the people who were at the synagogue that morning.'

'Where were you that morning?'

Molly was again taken unawares at this question.

'Why? Why do you want to know? Isn't it enough that I wasn't at the synagogue?'

'We don't know that,' Madison replied.

'You don't know that? I wasn't there. Ask anyone. Ask the secretaries.'

'Oh, I have. I have asked the secretaries and they both confirmed they hadn't seen you on the day. Which doesn't mean you were not there.'

Molly opened her mouth as if to speak and then closed it again.

'There are ways of getting into the synagogue without being seen by the secretaries.'

'There are?'

Madison observed Molly's reaction and had to admit to himself that he was probably barking up the wrong tree. The more he observed Molly, the more he was convinced that she was not sharp enough to be able to put on such a show of innocence. She looked genuinely surprised.

Madison decided that, as he was already there, he might as well pull another string and see where it led him.

'How do you get on with Miki Solomon?' he threw the question at her, then sat back to observe the effects of the change of subject.

Molly's face went a shade of red that Madison has not seen before. Blotches of red appeared on her cheeks, on her neck and even on her temples. Molly clearly felt herself going redder and redder and looked around as if trying to hide.

Madison's eyes fixed on her did not help the situation.

'How… what do you mean?' she managed finally, looking down at her hands, willing the redness to disappear.

'It was a simple question. How did you get on with Miki Solomon?'

'Has that got anything to do with the murder?'

'I was wondering the very same thing. Has it?'

'It's got absolutely nothing to do with it.'

Madison observed Molly in silence for a while.

'You are not comfortable talking about it,' he said at last.

'There is nothing to talk about,' she answered defiantly.

'On the contrary,' Madison said. 'From what I heard there is much to talk about.'

'Oh, really?' Molly found that being angry was a much better place to be. 'And who exactly were you talking to?'

'Miss Rubin,' Madison replied calmly, 'this is not how this is supposed to work. I am meant to ask the questions and you are meant to answer them.'

'You are a police officer,' Molly snapped. 'You should know better than listening to idle gossip.'

'On the contrary,' Madison persisted. 'Gossip is a treasure trove of information.'

Moly looked like a deflated balloon. She lifted her arm and looked at her watch, making sure Madison noticed her doing so.

Madison noticed.

'The better you answer my questions, the sooner you will get back to your job,' he said.

He saw Molly's shoulders drop in acceptance.

'I understand that at one time you were very close to Miss Solomon,' he started.

'Well, you understand wrongly. She was my teacher. That is as close as we got.'

'So, you don't like her?'

'I didn't say that.'

'You do like her then?'

'No, I don't. Honestly… what is this?'

'From what I gather,' Madison said after a pause, 'you helped Mr Kaufman get rid of Miss Solomon.'

'Nobody got rid of Miss Solomon. She resigned. You should get your facts right, Chief Inspector.'

The last two words were thrown at Madison with venom.

'Yes, she resigned, but only after you and Mr Kaufman made it impossible for her to stay.'

'That was Cecil's doing,' she protested. 'He did it. Not me.'

'But didn't you both make the complaint against her?'

'We did, yes. But I said we should complain to her. I didn't want him to go to the board about it.'

'Why not?'

Molly considered his question for a while and then replied softly.

'I never wanted her to go.'

Madison did not expect this reaction.

'You didn't?'

'No, I didn't.'

'But you and Mr Kaufman…'

'Mr Kaufman! Miss Solomon! Miss Rubin! Enough with all these silly titles. No one calls me Miss Rubin and no one calls Miki Miss Solomon.'

She stopped for a moment, but when nothing came back from Madison she continued.

'Mr Kaufman… Cecil… he took it too far. I never wanted it to go so far.'

'How far did you want to take it?'

'I don't know… I just wanted to put her in her place. She was walking around like the queen of Sheba, thinking no one could touch her… that she was so important, that everyone adored her. I just wanted to take her down a peg or two, that's all. But Cecil, he always knows – knew – best. He thought he could push her far and lord it over her. I told him that if he took it to the board, she would leave, but he never took any advice. He wanted to show her he was the boss… If he had a brain, he would have known that wouldn't work with her.'

'So that's why you hated Mr Kaufman?'

Molly turned around to look at Madison.

'Here we go again,' she said, more in contempt than in fear or frustration. 'I didn't kill him.'

And Madison finally had to admit to himself that in all probabilities she did not.

'Thank you for your patience, Miss Rubin,' he said, and walked out of the room.

39

DAY 12

The team was meeting in the incident room to exchange notes. Madison was standing by the big screen with the pointing stick in his hand. On the board was the list of all the suspects.

'What I want us to do now is exchange ideas and theories,' he said to his team. 'We will go down this list of suspects and I want each one of you to give us your opinion. Strong suspicion, unlikely, could be – anything you are thinking, I want you to share it with all of us. The four of us are very different. Different ages, different backgrounds, different outlooks on life… our suspects are also varied and different. We need to put our brains together and see what we come up with.'

His words were received with silence, but looking at the others, it was clear it was silence of approval.

'Right,' Madison started. 'The rabbi. Thoughts?'

The silence continued for a while.

'I know you like the rabbi, Jack.' Brodmann was the first to speak.

'I might like him but I don't rule him out as a suspect.'

'I don't quite see him as a suspect,' Benson said. 'What would be his reason? From what we hear, Kaufman tried it with him and failed. The rabbi himself told the board the whole story and completely disarmed Kaufman. He had already won. What would be the point of doing something like this when Kaufman was no longer a threat?'

'I agree,' Lisa said. 'He probably had the opportunity because no one noticed whether he left his room or not, but he had no motive.'

'That's my point,' Brodmann commented. 'I really don't see why he would. In fact, by talking to the board and telling them the truth, he made Kaufman look bad and strengthened his own position. I don't believe he did it, aside from the fact that you wouldn't expect a rabbi to engage in murder!'

Madison was amused and did not hide it.

'So now he is a rabbi? A kosher one? A proper rabbi and therefore innocent?'

Brodmann clearly did not enjoy the joke and Madison moved on.

'However, I tend to agree. I can't see why he would have done anything so stupid. He is a clever man. If he ever kills anyone, I am sure he will have a better reason before the Lord!'

'Miss or Mrs Mosco,' he continued. 'What are we thinking?'

Everyone took a minute to consider it.

'I don't think she did it,' Benson said after a pause.

'You don't?' Madison was surprised. 'It was you who complained that we let her off too easily.'

'I did,' Benson agreed, 'but since then I haven't discovered a shadow of a motive. So she had money problems. Who doesn't? But she is low down in the synagogue's hierarchy. I don't think she was a big enough fish to interest Kaufman.'

The rest of the team nodded in agreement.

Madison pointed to the next person on the list.

'Jonson,' he said. 'What are we thinking here?'

Brodmann was quite adamant.

'No way,' he said. 'Why would he? Kaufman had nothing on him.'

'That we know of,' Lisa pointed out.

'You can say that about everyone we have discussed so far. Probably not, that we know of, unlikely. Fact is that at the end of the day we are not going to remove a single suspect from our list, because although we think they are innocent, we can't prove it.'

The team could not argue with that.

Brodmann was not done.

'Who's next? Ah, yes – Miki Solomon,' Brodmann continued. 'Anyone think she did it? Come on. Let's hear you.'

No one spoke.

'Or Jane? Really – you must suspect someone? Anyone?'

'Jane couldn't hurt a fly,' Lisa said.

'So – do we take her out of this list? Wouldn't it be great to narrow the list down a bit? All we are doing is adding names.'

Madison was about to calm his sergeant down when someone knocked at the door.

That was surprising. This was the first time anyone knocked on the door of the little incident room.

'Come in,' Madison called out.

The door opened and Becky Mosco popped her head through.

'Sorry,' she said. 'It's just… can I have a word with PC Benson?'

Benson stood up but Madison put his hand up to stop him.

'If it's something to do with the case, Miss Mosco, we would all like to hear it.'

Becky seemed unsure of herself.

'I don't know that it is to do with the case… I'm not at all sure I should be bothering you with it.'

'You are not,' Madison said, betraying a little impatience. 'Please come in. What is it?'

Becky walked in and it was very clear she was very uncomfortable. Gone was the vivacious, confident secretary.

'I really like Miki and I'm sure it's nonsense…'

In spite of himself, Madison felt his stomach muscles tightening.

'Have a seat, Miss Mosco,' he said, trying to sound unbothered.

'Becky, please. No one calls me Miss anything… and it's Mrs anyhow.'

'Becky,' Madison corrected himself. 'Please sit down.'

Benson stood up, as there were no spare chairs in the little incident room.

Becky thanked him and sat down.

'It's just…' she started. 'I suddenly remembered something. It didn't mean anything at the time but you said to tell you anything about that day…'

Benson was standing next to her, having vacated his chair.

'Don't worry, Becky,' he said. 'What you say here is confidential.'

'I know… I've been telling myself it is stupid and to forget all about it, but it keeps nagging at me.'

In a comforting voice no one on the team expected from the young PC, Benson reassured her.

'Just spit it out, Becky,' he said softly. 'You will feel better afterwards.'

Madison liked what he saw. As Benson became more comfortable on the team and less awestruck by Madison, his qualities and contribution to the team became more evident.

A sharp brain, IT skills and, as was displayed at that moment, empathy and kindness.

'Well,' Becky started hesitantly, 'I didn't remember it when I talked to you.' She faced Benson. 'Only later did I realise I forgot something…'

Benson came closer to her.

'Take your time, Becky,' he said softly.

Madison turned his face to the window. He would not have told Becky to take her time – quite the opposite. He really needed to learn to control his impatience.

'Yes… it's probably nothing and I really like Miki. I'd hate to think… I don't want to get her into any trouble.'

'Why don't you tell us what it is you remembered, Becky?' Benson continued. 'We will decide whether it is something or nothing.'

'Right.' Becky looked like she might start crying. She turned towards Madison. 'I don't know why I didn't think of it when I spoke to PC Benson. It's just… when I told you that Miki was in and out of the synagogue… that she went into the synagogue to pick up her music, I forgot that after she said goodbye I happened to see her. I walked over to the kitchen to make a cup of coffee and I saw that her car was still there. I thought she had gone. She wasn't in the car and I guess I was a little curious, so I came out to see where she was. And then she came back to the car. She came from the direction of the side door. I think it was not locked because Jon had been carrying things out. He might have locked it… I don't know. I didn't check. I never gave it another thought.'

She stopped talking and the room was very quiet.

As this was 'his' witness, Benson felt empowered to be the first to speak.

'Thank you, Becky!' Benson started. 'That's very helpful.'

'How long?' Madison cut into Benson's speech.

'Sorry?' Madison's tone of voice was threatening and she became even more distressed. 'How do you mean?'

'How long between Miss Solomon leaving through the main doors and when you saw her coming back from the side door?'

'I see… I'm not sure. Like I said – I didn't think it was important, which is why I forgot all about it.'

'Was it five minutes? Ten? More?'

'I don't know… More than five, I think.'

'Ten? Fifteen?'

Becky clearly hated to be in this position, pointing a finger at someone she considered a friend.

'No… not as much as fifteen, I don't think.'

Everyone looked at Madison, expecting him to proceed, but he said nothing. He looked angry and Lisa thought he was being unfair on Becky, so after another glance at Madison, she decided to speak.

'Thank you, Becky. We appreciate it wasn't easy to tell us but you did the right thing.'

'Can I go now?' Becky asked, standing up.

Benson looked at Madison and, as no response came from him, replied to Becky.

'Sure. Thank you. We will let you know if… if we need to speak to you again.'

Becky rushed out of the room and Madison said nothing to stop her.

After a time when no one said anything and all eyes were on Madison, Brodmann, having known Madison longer than the rest of them, allowed himself to alert his friend.

'Jack?' he said, softly.

Madison looked at Brodmann as if he'd awakened him from a deep sleep.

'Well, Dave – you wanted someone to be a convincing suspect,' Lisa said, trying to defuse the tension in the room.

'The question is – why didn't she tell us?' Brodmann voiced what the rest were thinking. 'Miss Solomon. Why didn't she tell us she went back into the synagogue through the side door?'

No one spoke.

'I want to do a little experiment,' Madison said as he made his way towards the exit.

He stopped at the door and walked to the office. The two secretaries were at their desks.

'Can one of you please unlock the side door to the synagogue?'

He did not wait for a reply but walked back to join the others by the main door. He walked out, turned left and walked towards the side door and stood there, waiting for the rest of the team to follow him.

They heard the lock turn and watched the door open as Jane appeared in the doorway.

'Will this take long?' she asked. 'We don't like to leave the door open unless we are using it.'

'You can give Sergeant Brodmann here the keys. We will lock the door and return the keys to you when we finish.'

Jane handed the keys to Brodmann and could not disappear fast enough.

'Josh,' Madison said. 'Go to the car park. Lisa – you stand there, where you can see me here by the door as well as Josh in the car park. Dave will give Lisa a sign when he starts the timer on his phone and you then give Josh the sign to start walking towards the side door. Josh – you will walk fast, get in the door, walk up to the balcony, pretend you are pushing someone off the balcony, then come downstairs quickly, go out the door and walk to your car in the car park. Becky did not say Miss Solomon was running, so walk, but remember – you are younger and fitter than her, so don't walk too fast. Off you go.'

Benson disappeared around the corner. Brodmann was busy on his phone, opening the application. When he was ready, he signalled to Lisa, who then signalled to Benson. Soon, Benson appeared around the corner, walking at a steady pace but not too fast. He walked towards the side door, opened it and walked inside. Madison followed him in.

'Don't run up the stairs, Josh, but take it fairly fast.' Madison watched the balcony upstairs and soon Josh arrived.

'Now, walk down slowly and quietly till you reach the front of the balcony. That's good. Now – I imagine you would talk to him a little before the push because you couldn't possibly avoid being seen, so wait a bit. Do some talking. A little more. Now – push! Put some effort into it. He was quite a heavy man. Come on. Push harder!'

Benson was not a good actor. He never took part in any dramatic productions at school because he was too self-conscious, so he felt quite awkward fulfilling Madison's stage instructions. This was not something he practised at the police college. He felt really stupid pushing hard at the air above the balcony and was relieved when he was allowed to come down the stairs again and walk towards the exit door. He walked out and towards Madison's car in the car park.

Brodmann clicked his timer when Lisa motioned that Benson arrived at the car.

'Five minutes and a few seconds,' Brodmann called out. 'She would have had plenty of time to do it.'

40

DAY 13

Madison parked his car outside Miss Solomon's house. Lisa was sitting in the passenger seat. Neither of them spoke throughout the short drive from the synagogue.

'Leave the talking to me,' Madison said as they walked towards the bungalow.

Lisa had no intention of talking. She had never seen her boss in quite this mood and did not know what to make of it.

Madison knocked at the door and they were silent, waiting for Miss Solomon to open the door.

When she did, she looked really surprised.

'Chief Inspector,' she said. 'I didn't know… I didn't expect you.'

Madison replied, looking and sounding very stern.

'You have met PC Thompson, Miss Solomon. Can we come in?'

'Sure… come in.' She opened the door wide. 'I don't have long – I have a rehearsal soon.'

She closed the door behind them and led them into the living room.

'I wasn't told to expect you,' she said, turning to face Madison.

'I'm sorry,' Madison said. 'Something came up.'

The atmosphere in the room was icy.

'What? What came up?'

She suddenly noticed they were all standing in the middle of the room.

'Sorry,' she said. 'Please sit down.'

Lisa sat down and took out her notebook. Miss Solomon sat down opposite her, but Madison remained standing, which made both women feel very uncomfortable.

Madison got to business without further delay.

'When we last talked to you, Miss Solomon, you did not tell us that after departing the synagogue from the front, on the day of the murder, you then walked back into the synagogue through the side door.'

Miss Solomon was shocked.

'I what?' she asked, then continued. 'Oh, yes. I remember – I went to my car and then remembered that there was a piece of music I left on the piano, so I rushed back. The door was open so I grabbed the music and went back.'

Madison stared at her, clearly furious.

'Why didn't you tell me that?'

'I don't know… I honestly didn't remember… I'm sure if I had I would've told you.'

Lisa stared at Madison, wishing he would at least sit down, but he remained standing.

'How long were you there?'

'Sorry?'

'You went back into the synagogue through the side door. How long were you there?'

'The piano stands right by the door. I rushed in, took the music and rushed out… I couldn't have been more than two or three minutes.'

'Are you sure? Are you sure you didn't take longer than that?'

'I didn't time myself!' Miss Solomon said, less worried now and getting angrier.

'Clearly not,' Madison snapped. 'Because from what I hear, you were quite a bit longer than two minutes.'

Miss Solomon looked at Madison, perplexed.

'From what you hear?' she wondered. 'Oh, Becky… Becky saw me. Did she say I took longer than—'

'You don't expect me to answer that, do you?'

Lisa looked up at Madison, trying to signal her disapproval.

'I resent your attitude, Chief Inspector.' Miki was clearly upset. 'Are you accusing me of lying?'

'Well, you did not tell me the truth, did you?' he replied sharply.

Lisa felt she had to interrupt.

'Gov,' she said, not knowing what she was going to say. Luckily for her, at that point Madison's phone rang.

'Excuse me,' Madison said to the room at large. 'I have to take this.'

'Yes,' he barked into the phone.

He then listened for a while, his expression getting more tense.

'Something happened?' Lisa asked as he put the phone down.

'We have to leave,' he replied in Lisa's direction and started walking towards the door. He then stopped, almost crashing into Lisa, who was following him.

'You will find out sooner or later anyhow,' Madison said to Miss Solomon. 'Jon Jonson has been taken to hospital. He has had an accident.'

'Accident?' she said, her face ashen white. 'A car accident?'

'No,' Madison replied. 'There was an explosion in his caravan.'

With that, he moved towards the door.

'How… is he alright? How bad is he?'

Madison opened the door.

'It's not good,' he said to no one in particular, as he turned around and walked towards his car, with Lisa following, trying to match his long stride.

41

Once in the car, as Madison turned the car around and began to drive, Lisa could not hold back any longer.

'Sir,' she started. 'Jack – Gov – whatever I'm supposed to be calling you when we are in the car—'

'Jack would do!' he snapped.

'Jack, then. What the hell was that?'

'What the hell was what?'

'This. Your behaviour.'

'My behaviour?' Madison's voice contained a barely disguised warning.

'You were unnecessarily rude and antagonistic.'

'She did not tell the truth!'

'I'm not convinced of that. I can quite believe she forgot to mention it. She got to the car, remembered the music on the piano and rushed to get it. She was driving to the airport – everyone gets excited, tired, whatever – and she forgot. I can easily believe her.'

'Well – maybe you are more gullible than I am.'

'Maybe I am. But even so, Jack, I have seen you questioning suspects before. I never saw you treating them like this.'

'Like what exactly?'

Lisa stopped, as if wondering if she should be quiet or speak. In the end she opted to speak in a low voice.

'Like… it was a lover's tiff rather than a questioning of a witness or a suspect.'

Madison's foot hit the pedal and the car suddenly raced ahead. Very quickly his foot landed on the brake and the car jerked before he steadied it and continued driving.

Lisa thought that she envied Miss Solomon. She wished she could arouse such passion in her boss.

42

Back at the incident room, the team was assembled.

Madison informed his team of the latest events. He allowed them a few minutes to take in the news about Jonson.

Dave was the first to talk.

'Are we thinking this is connected to the murder of Mr Kaufman?'

'We don't know yet. It is a possibility we cannot disregard.'

'If it is,' Benson said, 'it would suggest that you were right, suspecting it all had something to do with Mr Kaufman's house.'

'If, Josh. If.'

'It could have been a simple gas explosion,' Dave said. 'Caravans invariably cook on gas. Right?'

'It could be, of course,' Madison agreed. 'The caravan is being examined as we speak. We will know more when they complete the examination, but I don't like coincidences. I'm going to go up to the Lakes immediately, to visit Jonson in hospital and hear from the Keswick police. Dave, will you come with me?'

Brodmann was about to speak but one look at Madison

changed his mind. He always knew when Madison needed him.

'Sure,' he said. 'I will just let Angi know.'

Brodmann took his phone out and walked out of the room.

'How is Jonson doing?' Lisa asked.

She did not look at Madison. She feared she had stepped over the line and did not want to see the look in his eyes when he replied.

'I understand he is in a bad way,' Madison replied, looking at her and noticing her reticence. 'The hospital made it clear over the phone that he is unlikely to be able to talk, but his daughter is on her way up from London. I want to talk to her.'

Lisa would have liked to accompany Madison. She thought she would be better suited to be talking to the daughter, but she guessed that, after her outburst in the car, Madison would not wish for her to join him on the long drive to Keswick.

When will you learn to keep your mouth shut, she told herself. She worried that Madison would never again choose her to be on his team. She could have kicked herself.

Brodmann came back into the room.

'That's fine,' he said. 'I will come with you.'

'Good.' Madison stood up. 'We will need some sustenance. Would you like to nip into the café and get us something? They make fantastic croissant sandwiches and great coffee.'

Brodmann did not need telling twice. He had heard all about the little café and could not wait to sample the goods.

'So we can go home for the night?' Josh asked.

'Sure. Thanks. I will see you here in the morning.'

Benson and Thompson stood up and started collecting their things.

'Lisa,' Madison said. 'Can you give me a moment?'

Benson went out of the room faster than he intended and Lisa stood there, hoping she did not show how upset she was.

'Lisa,' Madison said, 'you were right. My behaviour was unprofessional. You were right to point it out.'

The relief was so enormous that Lisa could not hold back her tears.

'I'm sorry,' she sobbed. 'I always speak before I think…'

'You were quite right to speak, Lisa.'

'I thought… you didn't ask me to come with you to Keswick and I thought… I thought you wouldn't want me on your team again.'

Madison smiled. He walked over to Lisa and put his arms around her.

'Now, now,' he said. 'I'm taking Dave because we go back a long way, and having him in the car with me for the drive is very natural. Go home and have a drink on me. You were right to say what you did and I will make sure to have you on my team in the future, so you keep me in check.'

Lisa smiled through her tears and picked up her coat.

'I will not let you down, Jack.'

And she ran out of the room.

43

'It was worth blowing Angi's dinner for this croissant,' Brodmann said, mouth full of the delightful sandwich.

'I am looking forward to having mine when we stop,' Madison said. 'This is a funny business, Dave, isn't it? It doesn't seem to be following any path that we recognise.'

Dave waited till he finished a mouthful.

'We certainly seem to be missing something here,' he said finally. 'I get the feeling that someone is having beginner's luck and flying under our radar.'

'You could be right, Dave. But I still can't shake off the feeling that it is all to do with Jonson's private access to the synagogue. Particularly if the explosion in the caravan was deliberate.'

With regret, Brodmann washed down the remains of the croissant with a cup of coffee, equally superior. He was definitely coming back for more.

'I have had a crazy idea,' he said.

'Good. We need some ideas. Crazy will do.'

'Well… what if the intended victim was Jonson all along?'

Madison kept his eyes on the road but mentally glanced at his sergeant.

'How?'

'Well, I did say it was crazy… I'm just thinking that, if someone wanted to kill Jonson, they could assume that anyone working at the synagogue when there were no activities there was the caretaker.'

'They don't look alike at all.'

'From the back you could be mistaken, especially if you were expecting Jonson to be there.'

'We don't know he was attacked from behind. In fact, the autopsy said he was hit on the side of the head. The attacker must have seen enough to know who he was hitting.'

'I'm clutching at straws, Jack,' Brodmann said. 'I'm trying to think outside the box. What if Kaufman was killed just in order to get us off the scent and that the one they really wanted to get was Jonson?'

Madison drove in silence for a while. Then, with a smile on his face he said, 'I didn't have you, Dave, as an Agatha Christie devotee!'

44

Madison and Brodmann arrived at the hospital in Keswick and were confronted with a chain of policemen guarding the entrance to the hospital.

Madison approached one of the policemen and presented his warrant card.

'DCI Madison and Sergeant Brodmann,' he said, pointing to Dave.

'Chief Inspector Brown is expecting you, sir. I will take you up to the ward,' the officer said, and led the way into the ward.

Madison and Brodmann followed the officer into the lift and up to the ward. As they walked out of the lift, a big man in a suit and tie walked towards them.

'Madison!' he exclaimed, and rather than shake the chief inspector's hand, grabbed him in a big bear hug.

'Arthur!' Madison said into the other man's jacket. 'What are you doing here?'

'Didn't they tell you I am in charge here?' Brown said, finally releasing Madison but holding onto his hand.

'The officer said Brown. I never connected.'

'I know. Not a very original name. I had asked my parents if we could change it but they were having none of it.'

He turned to Brodmann while still holding Madison's hand.

'He was my sergeant,' he said proudly. 'An arrogant whippersnapper but a brilliant officer.'

'This is Sergeant Brodmann,' Madison said, reluctantly. He loved his old boss but would have preferred not to have this nostalgic tour play in public.

Brown finally released Madison's hand and shook Brodmann's hand, heartily.

'Well – you are clearly not a whippersnapper but I'm sure you are a good officer or Jack wouldn't have you on his team.'

Chief Inspector Brown had a huge, booming voice and his laughter rolled down the corridor and towards the people waiting there.

Madison spoke softly.

'Arthur – how is Jonson doing?'

Brown got the message and his demeanour changed.

'I'm really sorry. It's just that I haven't seen you in such a long time. We should get together sometime,' he said, and proceeded to give Madison an overview of things.

'He has not gained consciousness. Has some internal damage. They are not too optimistic. I was hoping to be able to talk to him but as yet – no chance.'

'Have they finished examining the caravan?' Madison asked, matching his voice to Brown's softer tones.

'They did. There is no doubt. It was a deliberate act. Someone gained entry to the caravan and turned on the gas.'

Madison digested what he just heard.

'Was it a break-in?'

'No. Definitely not. No sign of damage to the lock or the door or any of the windows. Whoever did this had a key.'

For a while, no one spoke.

'Is his daughter here?'

'Yes. She is with him in room seven.'

'Have you told her what you just told me?'

Brown smiled.

'No. I thought I would leave that particular pleasure to you.'

'Right.' Madison started walking towards room number 7. 'What is her name?'

'I know her as Miss Jonson,' Brown said, walking alongside Madison.

Brodmann followed a little way behind the two chief inspectors.

45

Madison knocked gently on the door of room 7. A soft voice invited him to come in. He opened the door and saw a young woman sitting by the bed, holding her father's hand in her own. She turned to look at the door as Madison walked in, followed by the other two men.

'Miss Jonson,' he said. 'I am DCI Madison and I'm investigating the murder at the synagogue. This is Sergeant Brodmann, and you have already met Chief Inspector Brown. I'm really sorry to intrude, but – could we possibly talk to you for a few minutes?'

Miss Jonson let go of her father's hand and stood up.

'Sure,' she said. 'Can we do it somewhere else? I'm told he can't hear me but who knows? No one knows. I don't want to upset him.'

'There is a little nurses' room by the lifts. I already secured this room earlier on. We will not be interrupted there,' Brown said.

'I don't want to be long,' Miss Jonson said. 'I don't want him waking up when I'm out.'

'This won't take long, Miss Jonson. I promise you.'

'Miki!' Miss Jonson called out and waved.

Madison looked in the direction she waved to, and there was Miss Solomon hurrying up towards Miss Jonson.

'What is she doing here?' Madison said under his breath.

'Miss Jonson called her earlier and asked her to come here,' Brown replied.

The men stood there watching uncomfortably while the two women hugged and Miss Jonson broke down in tears.

'What… how is your dad?' Miss Solomon asked softly.

'Not good,' Miss Jonson replied through her tears. 'Look, Miki – these officers want to talk to me. Will you come in with me?' She turned to Madison. 'Can she come in with me?'

Madison noted the uneasy look Miss Solomon gave when she noticed him.

'Of course she can. We won't be long anyhow.'

The two women and the three officers made their way to the small nurses' room.

There were only three chairs there and Brodmann hurried out to get two more.

'I can't see why you want to talk to me at all,' Miss Jonson said. 'I can't see how I can help you.'

'Please sit down,' Madison said, pointing to the two chairs opposite his. 'This is what we do, Miss Jonson. We ask questions and occasionally we get an answer that helps.'

Brodmann came back into the room, carrying two chairs, and the three officers settled down, facing the two women.

'Miss Jonson,' Madison started, but did not get far.

'Oh, please,' Miss Jonson protested. 'Please just call me Sophie. It's like everyone is trying to remind me I have not yet found a husband.'

Miss Solomon put a hand on Sophie's arm, trying to calm her down.

'It's a stupid practice, anyhow. In the twenty-first century we are still changing our names to a man's name when we get married? How archaic is that?'

'Sophie,' Madison replied. 'I won't keep you long. Can you just tell me who has a key to your father's caravan?'

Sophie was not the only one in the room to look up at Madison in surprise.

'What?' she said, clearly confused.

'Do you have a key to the caravan?'

'I… yes. I do. I don't understand.'

'Apart from you and your father, does anyone else have a key?'

'I don't… No, I don't think so. Why?'

'Do you have the key on you? Now?'

'I think so… but… why do you want to know that? There was an explosion… gas explosion.'

Madison cut her off in a gentle but firm voice.

'Miss – Sophie,' he said. 'The explosion was not an accident. Someone gained entry to the caravan and turned on the gas. I am trying to find out who.'

Madison looked up and met Miss Solomon's look. She was clearly angry.

The room went silent.

'Someone… entered the caravan. I don't know what you mean?'

Sophie was hovering somewhere between fear and anger.

Chief Inspector Brown, who was the local officer and had all the information about the explosion, took over from Madison.

'Someone entered the caravan – with a key – and turned on the gas. Your father was a smoker, is that right?'

Madison and Brodmann had informed him that Jon was a smoker. He'd smoked during his interview with both officers.

Sophie nodded.

'It seems that he opened the door of the caravan – maybe already smoking or just lighting a cigarette – and that triggered the explosion. He did not even enter the caravan properly, which is why he was thrown outside.'

'But he surely would have smelt the gas, wouldn't he?' Miss Solomon wondered.

Sophie looked up, tears in her eyes.

'He had very poor sense of smell. He always blamed the smoking...'

Miss Solomon spoke very softly. 'Would you like some water?' she asked Sophie.

'Yes, thank you. I think I would.'

Miss Solomon stood up and left the room.

Madison stood up too.

'Dave – take over. I will be back in a minute,' he said, and walked out.

He caught up with her.

'Miss Solomon,' he said.

She turned to look at him. She was obviously furious.

'That was cruel,' she said.

'No,' Madison replied. 'That was not cruel. What was done to her father – that was cruel. What was done to Mr Kaufman – that was cruel. What will be done to one of you lot if I don't catch the person doing this soon – that would be cruel.'

Miss Solomon looked up at Madison.

'You really think?'

'Yes. I'm afraid I do.'

'I'm sorry—'

'No,' Madison said. 'I am sorry. I wanted to apologise for my behaviour earlier.'

Miss Solomon listened in amazement.

'It was unprofessional and unlike me,' Madison continued. 'My PC admonished me for that.'

'Good girl,' Miss Solomon said with feeling.

'She said something which made me examine myself,' Madison said, never taking his eyes of hers. 'She said it was more like a lover's tiff than a witness questioning.'

Miss Solomon, for once, was lost for words. She returned his look with a puzzled one.

'Meeting you was a bit of a shock. It awakened in me feelings I never thought I would have again… I don't normally allow my feelings to infringe on my work. When I found out you held back crucial information, I was very angry. With you, for letting me down, and with myself, because I had no right to expect anything from you.'

Neither of them spoke for a while.

'Can I assume,' Miss Solomon said, trying to hide the avalanche of emotions his words stirred in her, 'that I am no longer a suspect? Or you wouldn't be telling me this?'

'Please don't assume anything,' Madison replied. 'I will not allow any of what I just told you to get in the way of this investigation.'

Madison turned away from her and started walking back to the ward.

'Jack!' Miss Solomon called out. The use of his first name surprised him.

He turned around and walked back to her.

'For the record,' she said, 'the feeling is mutual.'

He looked straight at her, not a hint of a smile on his face.

'I know,' he said, and walked away.

She stood there for a while longer, looking after his disappearing figure.

'Arrogant bastard,' she said, and went in search of some water.

46

Madison returned to the nurses' room to find Sergeant Brodmann engaged in questioning that had moved far away from his own intended line of questioning.

Brodmann acknowledged Madison's arrival with a nod but continued his questioning. Madison sat back in his chair and listened to Brodmann without interfering.

'What is his name?' Brodmann continued.

Madison noticed that Sophie was looking more irritated than upset, as she was when he'd left the room.

'Bobby,' she answered, reluctantly. 'He has absolutely nothing to do with… with this.'

'Bobby what?' Brodmann asked, quietly.

'Bobby Granger,' she said. 'He is the kindest of people. He wouldn't hurt a fly. And definitely not my father. My father saved his life!'

'Did he?' Brodmann looked up, surprised. 'How?'

'I don't know a lot about it. I understand it was in the army. My father didn't like to talk about it but Bobby mentioned it once…'

'And yet, they haven't seen each other for a while?'

'I told you. This has nothing to do with… Bobby was like an uncle to me. He protected me. This is really silly.'

At this point Miss Solomon walked into the room with a glass of water. One look at her friend and she turned to the officers with a determined look.

'I think Sophie has had enough, officers' she said, and helped her friends to get up. 'If you need to speak to her again, you know where to find her. At her father's bedside.'

And with this she led Sophie out of the room.

Madison and Brodmann said their goodbyes to Chief Inspector Brown and did not speak until they were in the car, driving back towards Manchester.

The silence between them was uncomfortable and Brodmann was first to break it.

'I'm sorry, Jack, if I overstepped the mark,' he said. 'You left the room and I – where did you go anyhow?'

'You can follow your "hunch" if you like, Dave,' Madison said, concentrating on the road.

It was not lost on Brodmann that Madison did not answer his question, and he knew better than to persist.

'Wherever it is, make sure you contact the local police and ask for one of their officers to accompany you.'

'Of course, I will,' Brodmann replied, a tone of resentment in his voice. 'And where will you be?'

'I will be going back to Keswick. I want to talk to the camp manager and maybe to some of the regulars. They might have seen something. I will take Lisa with me.'

The rest of the drive passed in silence. Both men had a lot to think about.

47

DAY 14

The team had a short meeting the next morning to compare notes and plan the day. Brodmann and Benson were off to Stockport and Madison and Thompson were driving back to Keswick. They agreed to meet back at the synagogue in the early evening.

As Madison and Thompson were leaving the synagogue, they ran into the rabbi and his wife.

'Chief Inspector!' the rabbi exclaimed. 'I don't believe you have met my wife. Rachel, this is Chief Inspector Madison. Chief Inspector – my wife.'

Madison shook the rabbi's wife's hand – after a hesitation, as he was not sure about touching a Jewish woman's hand. He had had dealings with very Orthodox Jewish people in the past and he knew shaking hands with a woman was forbidden. However, anticipating his doubts, Rachel Zimmerman offered her hand to him and he shook it with relief.

'This is PC Thompson,' he said, introducing Lisa to Mrs Zimmerman. The two women also shook hands.

Rabbi Zimmerman turned to Madison, his face darkening suddenly.

'Chief Inspector,' he said, 'are we any nearer to knowing what is happening here? I'm afraid the congregation is in semi-panic mode. They are very worried, and frankly, I am too.'

Mrs Zimmerman cut into her husband's conversation.

'Ronnie, the Chief Inspector is leaving. Don't delay him.'

She turned to Madison.

'Could we talk to you sometime soon, Chief Inspector?'

'Sure,' Madison said. 'We should be back sometime early evening. I could call on you then, if you like?'

'That would be perfect,' Rachel said. 'In fact – why don't you come for dinner?'

Madison looked unsure and she got it.

'Well, you were going to come over to talk to us – which I'm sure is part of your job – and you would have to have dinner at some point this evening, so it would seem to make sense that we feed you while you do your job?'

Madison could see why the rabbi fell for this woman. Full of charm and charisma – not to mention very attractive.

'I promise you that this is not a bribery in any way,' Rachel continued, obviously enjoying the moment. 'I'm afraid my cooking is not that good.'

'Well – that's a relief!' Madison said, smiling. 'On those terms I would be honoured to accept.'

'And what about this young woman?' Rachel turned to Lisa. 'Would you join us also?'

'I… well… that's so kind,' Lisa said, 'but I'm afraid I already have something on this evening.'

'I am not quite sure what time I'll be back,' Madison said, 'but I will give you a warning before I appear.'

And with that the officers bade their farewells. Madison and Lisa walked to Madison's Yeti and Brodmann walked over to his car, where Benson had been waiting patiently.

48

Sergeant Sean Stewart was two months off retirement. Having spent the last two years 'pen pushing', according to himself, he was really looking forward to this assignment.

Brodmann was driving Benson and Sergeant Stewart, who was to accompany them when questioning Bobby Granger.

Sitting next to Brodmann, Sean Stewart could not stop talking.

'So, fill me in, Sergeant Brodmann,' he said. 'What's up with this lad, Bobby Granger?'

'Not so much of a lad,' Brodmann answered without much enthusiasm. 'And there is probably nothing up at all. It's routine. Just eliminating people.'

Sergeant Stewart could not hide his disappointment.

'It figures,' he said. 'Your boss is sending you on a wild goose chase and mine is also happy to be rid of me for the day!'

Brodmann was trying not to let Stewart get to him, but was finding it difficult.

'Actually,' he said, 'this is my idea. My wild goose chase.'

'Is it? Well – let's get you a result then. Take the next turn to the right. That's it. I used to live on this street. Know it like the back of my hand. What number did you say?'

'Number twenty-six,' Benson contributed from the back seat. He found the conversation between the two sergeants quite amusing.

Brodmann parked outside number 26.

Bobby Granger had done well for himself. He was living in a fairly large bungalow sitting on a big plot. Both Benson and Brodmann wondered about that. From what Sophie told them, he had been in the army with Jon. This house was in a different class to Jon's one.

The garden had a professional look about it. A gardener?

The door was opened very quickly after they knocked.

'Yes?' A guy appeared in the door, looking somewhat put off.

'Bobby Granger?' Brodmann said. He was about to present his warrant card when Sean Stewart pushed ahead of him. He flashed his card and almost pushed past Bobby Granger.

'Police!' he declared, and entered the bungalow.

'Police?' The blood drained from Bobby Granger's face. 'Why? What happened? Is it Jimmy? Mat? Are they…'

Brodmann rushed in after the two, trying to repair the damage.

'Mr Granger – nothing happened. I don't know who Jimmy or Mat are. It's nothing to do with them. Mr Granger!'

Bobby Granger stopped following Stewart into the house and turned to Brodmann.

'What is this about, officer? Who is in charge here?'

'I am, sir. I am in charge,' Brodmann said firmly. 'I'm sorry if we alarmed you. Jimmy and Mat are your boys? As far as we know, nothing happened to them. We are not here about your boys.'

Bobby Granger was looking from Stewart to Brodmann, trying to decide which one to address.

Then, turning his back on Stewart and through clenched

teeth, Bobby Granger said in a soft, angry tone, 'Get that Idiot out of my house!'

Stewart started to object but Brodmann raised his arm to stop him.

'Sergeant Stewart, can you please wait in the car?' Brodmann stretched his hand without looking at Stewart, and handed him the keys to the car.

Stewart thought about objecting but soon realised there was no point. He took the keys and went out.

'Thanks,' Granger said. 'Can you now tell me what this is all about?'

'We just need to ask you a few questions. About someone you used to know.'

The colour was slowly coming back to Bobby Granger's face, but he really wanted to sit down and have a drink.

'Come into the kitchen,' he said, leading the way.

He sat in one of the high chairs by the kitchen bar and motioned the officers to sit down also. He poured himself a glass of water and drank it, without offering them any.

Brodmann took the opportunity to look around the kitchen.

He didn't think he had ever been in such a luxurious kitchen. It was a big kitchen with an island in the middle. The units were white with a mirror-like finish, so that you could see your reflection in them many times, wherever you turned. No sign of the white goods – these were clearly hidden in a wash room.

There was a dining area – bigger than the whole of Brodmann's kitchen. A sofa and two armchairs in white, complementing the units, were arranged around a big wooden dining table with a glass top. Through the glass top you could see beautiful carvings on the wooden legs and frame of the table.

'So,' Granger said, putting his glass down. 'Why are you here?'

Brodmann was asking himself the same question. He was very confident when putting his case to Madison, but now, facing Bobby Granger, he suddenly wondered why he ever started on this road.

'I am sorry again, Mr Granger, for alarming you unnecessarily. We just came here to talk to you about Jon Jonson.'

Granger clearly did not expect that. He looked up at Brodmann and, for a time, could not find the words.

'We are talking to everyone who knew Jon,' Brodmann continued. 'We understand you were, at one time, very good friends.'

Hearing his own words out loud, Brodmann was beginning to wish that Madison had vetoed this venture before it started.

'Jon Jonson?' Granger finally found his voice. 'Why?'

Benson, who was leaning on the table taking notes, sensed Brodmann's hesitation and answered Granger's question.

'I'm afraid Mr Jonson has had a bad accident.'

'What kind of accident?'

'Gas explosion.'

'Gas explosion? Like… at home?'

'In his caravan.'

'Is he… is he alright?'

Brodmann came back in here.

'He is in a bad way,' he said. 'In hospital.'

Bobby Granger was looking from one officer to the other, struggling to understand.

'I…' he said after a while. 'I haven't seen Jon for over ten years. Did he mention me?'

'I'm afraid not, Mr Granger. He has not regained consciousness.'

Granger looked ever more puzzled.

'So… who told you about me? Was it… Sophie?'

Benson jumped in.

'We were asking her about everyone Jon knew.'

'Sophie must be devastated. Jon is all she has left of her family. Poor Sophie…'

'She is very upset,' Brodmann confirmed. 'Hopefully he will come out of it.'

'I still don't understand what you want with me? Like I said – we have not seen each other for years. I know nothing of his life these days.'

'But you used to be best friends, right?' Benson asked.

'Sophie told you that?' Granger did not wait for a response. 'Yes, we were. But that's history.'

'Can you tell us what happened?' Brodmann enquired.

Granger was getting angry again.

'Why the hell should I?' he snapped. 'It has nothing to do with what happened to Jon.'

'You are probably right, Mr Granger,' Benson agreed. 'But we have to cover all possibilities. You know – just to eliminate things.' He was borrowing from Brodmann's handbook.

Granger stared at Brodmann, as if trying to read answers off the sergeant's face.

'You said it was an accident. Right?'

'Well… in a manner of speaking.'

'It wasn't an accident?'

Benson looked up from his writings.

'No. It was not an accident.'

'Someone caused an explosion in Jon's caravan?'

'That's right.'

'And you think that was me?'

Brodmann was silently cursing Madison for giving him a long rope to hang himself with.

'Mr Granger. We are only doing our duty. We are only elimi—'

'Yes, you said. You are only eliminating me from your inquiry.'

Granger took his glass to the sink and refilled it.

'If you're looking for a motive,' Granger said finally, 'then I have one. But why would I wait so many years before acting on it?'

Brodmann did not reply and Benson took his cue from the sergeant. It seemed a good time to just let Granger open up in his own time.

'It was personal. I don't like talking about it,' Granger said reluctantly.

He waited for a reaction, but none came.

'I know what you are thinking, anyhow,' he said. 'You are looking at this kitchen and wondering how I could afford it.'

The sudden change of subject surprised the two officers.

'It is a beautiful kitchen,' Benson said after a little hesitation. 'My mother would die for one.'

'And we have no idea what you do for a living, Mr Granger,' Brodmann added. 'Why should we have any opinion about you being able to afford this lovely house?'

'Everybody does,' Granger said, revealing a huge chip on his shoulder. 'And I didn't earn it. If you must know, I won big on the lottery.'

Again Mr Granger managed to surprise the two officers.

'You didn't need to tell us that, Mr Granger. It is not our business.'

Granger returned to his chair and played with his glass for a while, before speaking.

'Jon and I were buddies from our army days. He saved my life. I owed him everything. When his wife died, we practically moved in. We looked after him and after Sophie, who was devastated. It was such a difficult time. Sophie used to call us Uncle Bobby and Aunty Jean. We were inseparable. A couple of years later I was rushed to hospital with appendicitis. There were complications and I ended up staying in the hospital for something like two months.'

Granger stopped talking and looked inside his glass. He clearly did not want to continue. The silence in the room was weighing heavily on him.

'Jon was good,' he said with effort. 'He looked after Jean and the boys the whole time I was ill. Soon after I got back, Jean couldn't take it anymore… She told me that while I was away, she had an affair with Jon… I never saw him since. My marriage was over. I see Jean when needed because of the boys, but otherwise – I don't see her. So, as you can see, I certainly have a motive…'

After a while, Brodmann stood up.

'I'm sorry to put you through this, Mr Granger,' he said. He'd started moving towards the kitchen door, with Benson following him, when he stopped and turned back to look at Granger.

'Just one more thing, Mr Granger,' he said, carefully. 'What were you doing on Sunday afternoon, between two and four?'

Granger stood up and stared at Brodmann.

'Are you kidding me?' he asked.

'I'm sorry, Mr Granger. I have to ask.'

'Your case must be pathetic if you are coming after me.'

Brodmann thought Granger had no idea how right he was.

'If you just answer this question, we will be out of here and leave you in peace.'

'I was at a gig at the rugby club.' Granger practically hissed this out. 'Mat – my youngest – is in a band. They were playing all day.'

'Anyone who can verify this?' Brodmann asked out of habit, knowing it was a silly question.

‘Only the whole club, my sons, my ex and the band. Oh, and the barman who had to tell me I’d had one too many.’

At the door, Granger asked in a much softer tone, ‘Which hospital is Jon in?’

Benson took a page out of his notebook and quickly scribbled the address.

49

The manager of the campsite was waiting for them when they arrived.

'DCI Madison?' he enquired, offering his hand to him.

'It is,' Madison confirmed, 'and this is PC Thompson.'

'Blake Williams,' the manager announced, and shook Lisa's hand. 'Come into the office.'

He led the two officers into his office where two chairs were ready, facing the table behind which Blake Williams now took his seat.

'Can I get you anything to drink?' he asked the two officers.

They had stopped on the way for a bite of lunch, so politely turned down the offer.

'So,' Williams started, leaning back on his recliner chair. 'We have never had anything like this happen before. People are leaving in droves. Some have been with us for years but they are moving their vans to another site. This could run me out of business.'

'The sooner we find out what happened here, the sooner you can reassure them that they can bring their vans back.'

'I am all for that. Tell me what I can do.'

'For starters, you can answer my questions.'

Williams leant forwards on his table.

'Ask away. Please. If I can help in any way, please let me know.'

'Ok,' Madison said, noting that Lisa was at the ready with her notebook. 'Jon Jonson. You knew him well?'

'I knew him,' Williams said. 'Not very well. He is just one of the regular weekenders. We say hi and sometimes he will ask for help with something… so I wouldn't say I knew him very well.'

'And he was in the habit of coming every Sunday?'

'Like a clock. About three p.m. on a Sunday.'

'Does he mingle with your regulars?'

'I can't really say.'

Williams stopped for a moment, concentrating.

'There is a couple to the left of his caravan,' he said. 'June and Rafe. I have spotted them chatting a few times – as you do in a campsite. But I'm not sure there was more to it than that.'

Madison thought for a minute.

'Does anyone use Jon's caravan when he is not there? Like family? Friends? Maybe during the week?'

'I don't think so. Not that I have ever seen.'

'Do you have a key to Jon's caravan?'

'Me? No. What for? If I need to move a caravan – which hardly ever happens – I can do it without getting inside.'

Like so many times while investigating this case, Madison was getting nowhere fast.

Williams looked at the chief inspector with concern.

'Are you saying that someone got into Jon's caravan and caused the explosion?'

'It's looking like that, yes,' Madison admitted.

'So – it wasn't just an accident?'

'Not an accident. No.'

'Murder?'

Williams was pondering this information.

'I can't decide,' he said finally, 'what is worse for the business. An accidental gas explosion or a deliberate one. Either way, we are doomed.'

'It doesn't have to be like that, Mr Williams. If we find out who did it and arrest them, your people should come back after a time.'

'This is really strange… Why would anyone? This is why you were asking all these questions?'

'Yes. It would help us to know who had a key to Mr Jonson's caravan.'

'How would I know? I don't spy on my campers. They come and go as they please. I didn't get the impression that anyone ever used the caravan in Mr Jonson's absence. Not even his girlfriend.'

Lisa looked up from her notebook. She and Madison exchanged looks before Madison said, keeping his voice steady, 'Girlfriend?'

'Like I said – I don't spy, but from what I could see, she never arrived before him so I don't know if she had a key or not.'

Madison was careful not to raise his voice, although his pulse increased and he wondered if Williams could hear his heartbeat.

'Mr Jonson has a girlfriend who comes to visit him in the caravan?' he asked very softly.

'Yes,' Williams answered, sounding surprised. 'You didn't know?'

Madison suddenly felt really stupid. Why didn't they know?

'She has been visiting him for years. Practically every Sunday that I could tell. You don't think…?'

'You have a name for her?' Madison asked.

'Ah… sorry… that I don't have. The caravan pitch is registered under Jonson's name. That is all I need to know. I don't think I ever talked to her. Live and let live is my motto.'

Lisa stopped writing. She looked at Madison, and when he did not seem to be ready to ask, she took the initiative.

'How did she arrive here? On Sundays? Did you ever see her arriving?'

'Yes, I did. She drove here.'

The two officers sighed soundlessly. Something to get their teeth into.

'What car did she drive?'

Williams scratched his head.

'Can't say that I particularly noticed. It was a little red one. Maybe a Fiat? Or a Citroën? We get so many cars here and I'm only interested in cars that can tow caravans. And sports cars.'

Madison looked around the office.

'Any CCTV?'

'Ah. Kind of.'

'Kind of? What does that mean?'

'It's an old system. The video is not very clear.'

'How often do you wipe it?'

'I try to do it every couple of months. Don't always succeed.'

'So, when was the last time?'

'Sunday morning.'

'This last Sunday?'

Madison wanted to kick someone, or at least something.

'Yes. I was late doing it. Sorry. How was I to know that someone was going to get murdered in my campsite?'

'But it was working on Sunday?'

'It should have been. Like I said, it is not very reliable.'

'Still – I would like to have a look.'

Williams took the disc out of the CCTV and put it into the player.

'Do you want to watch the whole day?' he asked.

'I'm afraid we will have to,' Madison said. He was quite looking forward to dinner with the rabbi and his wife and was hoping this would not take too long.

'Your eyes are younger than mine,' Madison told Thompson. 'We are looking for a little red car – something like a Citroën.'

'Yes, Jack. I heard him.'

'We might see someone breaking into the caravan.'

The two officers remained in the campsite office, watching, and rewatching if they thought they might have missed something. Williams kindly brought a few cups of coffee and even some biscuits.

Madison picked up his latest cup of coffee and stood up.

'I'm going out for a bit of fresh air. My eyes need a rest,' he said. 'Are you joining me?'

'I'm OK for now, Jack,' Lisa said. 'If you trust me to do this on my own, I will carry on.'

Madison walked out. He leant on a tree, drank his coffee and took in the smell of the woods. He used to go camping with his family when he was young. The smell was so poignant, he could close his eyes and smell the BBQ his father always prepared for the family's dinner. There was a time when he was enjoying planning to take his own children camping too.

Madison shook his head and opened his eyes. He was not a natural daydreamer and he rejected the temptation to indulge in fantasies.

The mysterious girlfriend intrigued him. No one ever mentioned a girlfriend. Wouldn't Sophie have said something? Surely, she would have wanted to let her know. Did Jon meet his girlfriend only at the campsite? Never at his home? And where was she? She always came on Sundays, according to Williams. Did she know what happened to Jon?

So many questions.

'Jack!' Thompson called from inside the office.

Madison hurried back inside.

'Do you think this is the car?' she asked, pointing to the screen.

Madison sat back in his chair and studied the screen carefully.

Thompson rewound the tape and played again the car arriving into the field of vision of the camera. The car continued for a while and then stopped.

'Can you see who is in the car?' Madison asked.

'No. The sun is shining directly on the front screen.'

'Mr Williams?' Madison called out.

Williams came in and as soon as he caught a glimpse of the screen he confirmed.

'That's her,' he said. 'That's the car.'

As a matter of fact, the car was a Nissan Micra. Close enough.

The three continued watching the tape. The car stopped for a while. No one came out. They watched for about seven minutes before the car started moving. It turned around slowly and drove away.

For a while the room was silent.

'What the hell?' Williams said.

'Lisa,' Madison asked, ignoring Williams, 'what time did she arrive?'

Thompson wound the tape back and watched the car arriving again.

'Four twenty-three p.m.,' she said.

'Four twenty-three,' Madison repeated. 'And the explosion was at three forty-four. Look at the direction the car is pointing. She was nearly at the caravan. She saw what had happened and she just turned back and left.'

‘Maybe she just came to check?’ Thompson offered. ‘Maybe she knew what would happen and just wanted to know everything worked alright?’

‘You’re not serious. Are you?’ Williams was horrified. ‘She is a nice lady. She wouldn’t…’

‘Stop the tape,’ Madison commanded and Lisa stopped the tape. On the screen the back of the car was facing the camera and, although not the clearest of pictures, the registration number was quite readable.

Lisa put the number in her notebook. The two officers thanked Williams and left the office.

In the car, Madison got on the phone to head office and gave the details of the car. It didn’t take them long to get back to him with the name, telephone number and address of the driver of the red Nissan Micra.

50

Madison got off the phone.

'Her name is Nina Gibson,' he said. 'She lives about half an hour away from here.'

'Are we going to see her?' Thompson asked.

'That's the plan, but we have to be careful. We can't just show up on her doorstep. We don't know the reason for the secrecy. Obviously, if she did this, all will be revealed anyhow, but just in case she didn't, we have to respect her privacy.'

'So how are we playing this?'

Madison thought for a while.

'I have her mobile number,' he said. 'I think, in the first instance, I will call her.'

The two officers were still in the car park of the campsite. They sat in silence for a while longer, while Madison was thinking ahead to his conversation with Nina Gibson. At last, he picked up his mobile phone and dialled. He then put the phone on speaker.

The two officers listened to the phone ringing at the other end with increasing dread. Nina was clearly not answering the phone.

Madison gave it three more minutes and tried again. He let the phone ring for a while when, surprising him, Nina picked up the call.

'Hello?' She was barely heard over the speaker.

Madison sat up in his seat.

'Nina'? he asked. 'Nina Gibson?'

'Who is this?' she asked in a resigned voice, as if she already knew.

'DCI Madison of the Manchester police,' he replied.

'Manchester?' She sounded confused.

'Can I come and see you?' Madison pressed on.

She replied almost in a whisper, as if trying not to be heard. 'Is it about Jon?'

'It is. I could be with you in twenty minutes.'

'No, no. Please – don't come here.' The panic in her voice was palpable. 'There is a park at the bottom of the main road. I could be there in twenty minutes. Please meet me there.'

Madison agreed. He had her address and she knew it. She was clearly desperate to stop them from coming to the house, so he was quite certain she would meet them at the park.

'There is a café down the path from the entrance,' she said. 'I will meet you there.'

Madison waved to Williams, who was watching them from the window of his office, and started the engine. He knew Williams would be relieved to see them go. Although his beloved green Yeti was not a police car, his presence in the campsite had been noted by the regulars and was making them nervous.

'This is very mysterious,' Lisa said when they started on their way to meet Nina. 'All this secrecy around their relationship. He was free and so no need for him to be shy about it. It must be her. She must be married. Is her husband dangerous? Does he beat her up?'

'We will find out soon enough,' Madison answered.

'She probably saw what happened. She either saw the van on fire, or after – when the fire was put out and there was almost nothing left of it. She might even have seen Jon on the ground. And what does she do? She turns the car around and scarpers. How suspicious is that?'

Madison did not bother to answer. Nina's behaviour was beyond strange. He was keen to get to the bottom of it.

The journey took a little longer and it was more like thirty minutes by the time they arrived at the park café.

A woman was sitting outside the café at a table for four. She stood up hesitantly when she saw them. Madison walked towards her and offered his hand.

'Nina Gibson?' he asked.

'Yes,' she replied, and shook his hand.

'DCI Madison, and this is PC Thompson,' he said, flashing his warrant card. Thompson did the same.

They all sat down and Thompson took out her notebook.

'Do I address you as Miss or Mrs or Ms Gibson?' Madison started.

'Just call me Nina,' she replied, and Madison was wondering why they always insisted on giving their witnesses and suspects a title. Most of them preferred to be addressed by their first name.

Madison studied Nina carefully. She was not what anyone would imagine a secret lover to look like. She looked like your regular, kind neighbour. She was on the skinny side of thin. Her hair was greying but still revealed its blonde origins. Her complexion was good considering she must be in her late fifties.

'How is Jon?' she asked in a barely heard voice. She was clearly close to tears.

'He is not good,' Madison replied, watching her tentatively. 'You know of his… accident?'

'Yes,' she whispered.

'You didn't come to see him in the hospital.' Madison presented it as a question.

'No. I didn't.'

'However – you were there on Sunday.'

'What? I wasn't…'

'There is no point denying this, Nina. The campsite has a CCTV system. We saw you arriving, then turning around and driving away.'

Nina was surprised but quickly relented.

'I drove in and then I saw a lot of people standing around where the caravan was supposed to be… I stayed for a little bit. I saw someone on the ground and people around him… I thought it must be Jon but people were taking care of him, so I left.'

'Why, Nina?' Madison sounded more patient than he felt. 'Why did you not stay with Jon?'

Nina was folding and unfolding her napkin. She barely touched the cup of coffee in front of her.

'You think… you think it wasn't an accident?'

'What makes you say that, Nina?'

'Well… why would you be investigating it if it was just an accident?'

'You are quite right,' Madison replied. 'This was not an accident. We are investigating anyone who had anything to do with Jon, and clearly you were the closest to him, yet no one knew about you, and you ran away instead of rushing to Jon's bedside. We find this intriguing.'

Nina was silent for a few moments. She clearly intended to talk but was trying to decide where to start. The two officers allowed her the time she needed.

'Jon and I,' she started, still looking down at her napkin, 'have been… together for a few years. We met years ago when both our families were camping. We had lost touch when we happened to bump into each other in a shopping centre. We became very close… my husband and I had drifted away from each other. There was nothing left in the marriage and I was going to leave him and go and live with Jon but… my husband became ill. He has cancer. I couldn't leave him. Jon understood. I stayed with my husband and only saw Jon on Sundays. My sister comes to look after Darren every Sunday so I can have a break. She doesn't even know about Jon… no one knows. I didn't, don't, want Darren to find out about it. If he knew I had intended to leave him but stayed because of his illness, he would be so hurt… He is a very proud man.'

Nina stopped talking and Madison had run out of questions. This was not what he was expecting. A jealous, violent husband who terrified her would have made more sense.

As if reading his thoughts, Nina looked at Madison and answered his unspoken question.

'Darren is a lovely man,' she said with a little sad smile on her face. 'We are really good friends and always have been. If I ever loved him in the way… the way a woman loves a man, it died a long time ago. When I planned on leaving him, he was in his prime. Women always liked him. I thought he would not have a problem replacing me, but then came the cancer… Darren finds it hard letting me nurse him, but if he knew about Jon… I am sure he would tell me to leave. He would not let me help him. There is no one else. The kids are far away and there is no one who would be prepared to be here day in and day out. I could not forgive myself if he found out.'

Madison was moved by this. He could see that Lisa was too.

No one spoke for a while. Nina was the first to break the silence.

'I wonder…' She looked at Thompson when she spoke, automatically appealing to the woman officer. 'Could you let me know… how Jon is doing? I know it's a lot to ask.'

Thompson was about to reply when Madison's phone started ringing. Madison looked at the phone and stood up.

'Forgive me,' he said to no one in particular. 'I have to take this.'

He moved away, far enough to be out of earshot, and picked up the call.

'Rabbi,' he said. He looked at his watch at the same time. He was probably going to be late to the dinner. 'What can I do for you?'

The rabbi started talking and Madison stopped in his tracks. He listened for a few minutes and then just said, 'Thanks for letting me know,' and put the phone down. He stood for a while, undecided, and then called up to Thompson.

'Lisa,' he called out. 'Can you come here a minute?'

Lisa, who was talking with Nina, excused herself and left the table. She joined Madison and could see on his face that something bad had happened.

'Lisa,' he said softly. 'That was the rabbi on the phone. He just had a call from the hospital. Jon is dead.'

Thompson looked at Madison but could not speak. She glanced at Nina, still sitting by the table, and back at Madison.

'God,' she finally whispered. 'How awful.'

Madison remained silent.

'What… what are we going to do?' she asked.

'We have to tell her,' Madison said.

'Oh, no… we can't…'

'We have to,' Madison insisted. 'She has to be told. I'm just wondering… could you stay with her for a while… if she wants you to? I will make sure someone picks you up.'

'Of course I will,' Lisa said.

She glanced at Nina again. Nina was not looking in their direction. She seemed to be in a world of her own.

'Do you want me to tell her?' she asked, dreading the answer.

'No. I will tell her. You just be there for her.'

And with that the two turned and walked back to the table.

Nina looked up as they approached the table and knew immediately.

'Is it Jon?' she asked in a calm, resigned voice.

Thompson sat down next to her and took her hand. Madison sat down across from the two women and answered.

'I'm afraid it is, Nina,' he said. 'I'm so sorry.'

Lisa held Nina's hand tighter.

'I'm so sorry, Nina. So sorry.'

Nina stood up.

'I'm afraid I have to go home,' she said in an eerily normal voice. 'I have to get Darren's dinner.'

'Don't go yet,' Lisa pleaded. 'Let me get you another drink. Take your time. I will stay with you.'

'No. I have to go.'

'But… you can't go like that. You shouldn't be on your own right now. Let me come home with you. Maybe I can talk to your sister?'

'No!' Nina was more determined than they thought her capable of. 'I'll be OK.' She looked at the officers as if she was comforting them.

'I have lived this scenario many times before,' she said calmly, patting Lisa's hand. 'In my mind, I have lost him so many times already. Every time he was driving up to the caravan I was wondering – what if he doesn't make it? What if he is killed on the road? What if he has a heart attack? And what if he has an accident on his way back? No one would let me know. I would have no idea until I arrived at the caravan the following Sunday… and even then, I would not have a way of knowing. At least this way I know.'

'But… we can't leave you. It's not right.' Lisa could not find the words.

'I will be OK,' Nina assured her. 'The boys are coming home at the weekend… a lot to do… I will be very busy.'

She started walking away and then, as if she remembered, she turned around and spoke to Madison.

'Can I ask one thing?'

'Of course. What is it?'

'If you could let me know when and where the funeral will be? I will not come but I would like to visit when everyone has gone… on my own. It always was on my own…'

'Of course,' Madison said. 'As soon as I know I will let you know.'

51

The roads were not busy and Madison was making good progress. They had been driving for ten minutes in silence. Lisa's head was turned away from him, as she was trying to hide how upset she was.

After a while, Madison took a handkerchief out of his pocket and handed it to her.

'It is clean,' he said. 'It has been crumpled in my pocket, but it is clean.'

Lisa took the handkerchief and wiped her eyes. This little kindness only made her less able to control her emotions.

'I'm sorry,' she said. She was trying to speak in her normal voice but without success.

'Don't apologise for having a heart!' Madison said. 'Too many people in the job lose their humanity. Try not to lose yours.'

'I can't get her out of my mind.' Lisa was sobbing gently. 'Carrying on looking after her husband… telling no one… mourning in silence. It's too cruel.'

'And yet,' Madison continued, 'you have to pick yourself up, wipe your eyes and blow your nose, and continue working on an investigation where Nina is still very much a suspect.'

Lisa looked at Madison in amazement.

'You can't think that? After everything you heard?'

'What did we hear? We heard what Nina wanted us to hear. We will never hear Jon's side of the story. We have no idea how things really were between them. Her behaviour is strange, to say the least. Yes, the sick husband she is looking after can explain some of it, but it could also be a screen. She didn't want you coming anywhere near the house. Who knows what you might have found if you went to the house?'

Lisa sat there for a while, unable to say a word.

'I'm not sure I'm cut out for this job,' she said at last. It was the first time she had expressed a doubt about her chosen profession.

Madison laughed.

'I can't tell you how many times in my life I have asked myself the same question,' he said. 'I still ask it these days. I can't tell you at what stage you will be sure you have chosen the right career. I don't know if you ever get there. But I do know that if you don't have doubts about your job, you are probably not very good at it.'

They continued to drive in silence.

After a while, Lisa blew her nose into the handkerchief.

'I will give it back to you. After washing it.'

'I'm relieved to hear it,' Madison said.

'My mother always told me to make sure I have a clean handkerchief in my bag,' Lisa said, smiling through her drying tears.

'They know what they are talking about, mothers,' Madison said.

52

'I will be quite a lot later than we agreed.' Madison was speaking into his phone after dropping Lisa at the synagogue's car park, where she'd left her moped. 'Maybe we should reschedule.'

'It is not too late for us, Chief Inspector,' the rabbi answered. 'Please come.'

'Are you sure?' Madison protested. 'What with the terrible news…'

'It's because of the terrible news that we want to talk to you even more, Chief Inspector. And Rachel really made an effort.'

'OK,' Madison said, admitting to himself that he was really hungry and any food – even from the kitchen of Rachel Zimmerman, a self-confessed mediocre cook – would be welcome.

53

As it happened, the meal was really quite good. Rachel – Rochalé as the rabbi fondly called her – made what she claimed was a typical Friday night dinner. Fish cakes for starter, chicken soup, and then roast chicken with roast potatoes and carrots. Madison was surprised how much he enjoyed the meal. He had just a little wine which the rabbi used for the kiddush – a prayer said before the meal.

The conversation was flowing easily and Madison realised it would be very easy to let his guard down with this couple. It was almost tempting, to unburden himself to them. He could see how people would feel comfortable bringing their problems to either one of this power couple. Madison resisted. Both the rabbi and his wife were still on the suspect list.

'I am waiting to hear from Sophie,' the rabbi said as they retired from the dining room to the living room. 'She is driving down from Cumbria and will stay at her father's house for one night. Miki will let me know when they arrive and I intend to go over for a short time. She is not Jewish but I would like to offer her support nevertheless.'

Madison was choosing his words carefully.

'Is Sophie very close to Miss… to Miki?'

'I don't think so,' Rochalé replied. 'Not very close.'

'And yet, she is with Sophie at the hospital now.'

'I don't think Sophie knows many people at the synagogue. She has been in London for quite a few years. She was up a while ago when she was worried about her father. She came to the synagogue and wanted to talk to someone and Miki happened to be there, so she confided in her.'

'She was worried about her father?' Madison enquired.

'I have no idea what it was about,' Rochalé replied. 'I think he went away on holiday without telling Sophie and she couldn't contact him. She came up here and that's when they met.'

'I might warn you, Chief Inspector,' the rabbi said with a cheeky smile aimed at his wife, 'that in this house a bad word against Miki Solomon is not allowed!'

'Why the warning?' Rochalé protested. 'Was the chief inspector about to say something bad about Miki?'

The rabbi found it all quite amusing.

'My dear,' he said, 'the chief inspector is here to listen, not to reveal.'

'That is not fair,' Madison said, finding it impossible not to like the rabbi and his wife. 'I understood I was here to be fed – and I was. Admirably so.'

Rochalé smiled and bowed her head in acknowledgement.

'Coffee, Chief Inspector?' the rabbi asked. 'We have allocated duties in this house. Rachel does the cooking and I do the coffee.'

Madison felt like suggesting they call him Jack, but he did not want to encourage overfamiliarity at this stage.

'Coffee would be very nice, thank you, Rabbi.'

Rabbi Zimmerman left the room and Madison found himself alone with the delightful Rochalé.

'BTW, Chief Inspector – don't bother to try and pronounce

the name Ronnie calls me. My name is Rachel. Always has been. It's only Ronnie that insists on calling me Rochalé. It's a kind of a nickname. It's a very Jewish, *Fiddler on the Roof* kind of a name, but it does have an element of fondness in it.'

'Thank you for this,' Madison said, clearly amused. 'I must admit I am relieved.'

'The addition of "lé" at the end of a name expresses fondness. But not every name goes well with it. For instance – Rachel. Rachelle' sounds awful. Rochalé works well. Your name is Jack. Right? It wouldn't work with Jack. Jacklé just doesn't roll off the tongue. Jack is Jacob and Jacob in Hebrew is Ya'akov – but the nickname would be Yankalé.'

Rachel examined Madison carefully, then laughed.

'You don't look like a Yankalé,' she said. 'Any more than I look like a Rochalé. But one day if someone Jewish likes you very much they might want to call you Yankalé.'

'Not much chance of that,' Madison replied quickly, and changed the subject speedily.

'Where in America do you come from?' he asked.

'New York. Born and bred.'

'It must have been quite a cultural shock, moving from New York to this small-town institution.'

'Yes and no,' Rachel replied. 'In some ways – yes. New York has everything, from concert halls to theatres to malls to Fifth Avenue to Central Park… but when you are a Jew, in a way you are always living a small-town kind of life. It's what happens in the synagogue that rules your life. Much like here.'

'But I think American Jews must be different to English Jews.'

Rachel helped herself to a few nuts on the table, while considering the question.

'I am not the best person to judge,' she said at last. 'I think Ronnie told you the circumstances of our getting together… So over there I was seen as a wicked woman, whereas over here, I am the wife of a very popular rabbi. But if I try to find differences, I would say that the politics of the synagogue are different. You would be surprised to hear this, in view of what I just told you about how I was viewed, but I think the politics of the synagogue here are possibly even more "political". The Americans, on the whole, are more open with their politics. It's out there. Here they pretend that politics don't exist. There is a cover-up of politeness and good manners, but if anything, it is more vicious.'

At this point the rabbi entered the room, wheeling a trolly with a cafetière, cups and plates with cookies on them. The rabbi clearly caught the tail end of the conversation.

'Rochalé,' he said, 'the chief inspector is not interested in the politics of the synagogue.'

'You'd be surprised,' Madison said.

Rachel confronted her husband.

'If the chief inspector is to solve these awful murders,' she challenged, 'he has to understand the psychological make-up of this community.'

'Milk?' the rabbi asked.

'No, thanks,' Madison replied. 'Just as it comes. No milk, no sugar.'

For a few moments only the sound of cups and spoons and liquid being poured could be heard.

'I must confess that I am not intimately involved with any religious institutions.' Madison was the first to break the silence. 'Let alone a Jewish one. So, anything you can tell me which will throw some light on things would be welcome.'

'Took me a while to learn how it works over here,' Rachel said. 'Sometimes I am still baffled. The board runs the place, but does it quite secretly. From where I'm sitting, most people who put themselves up for the board do it to fulfil something that is missing in their lives. There are some – very few – who do it for the genuine care for the community and the survival of this synagogue. But for most, it is reaching the heights they cannot reach in the outside world.'

'This is a little harsh,' the rabbi said. 'As you can see, the rabbi's wife does not look for the best in people.' He gave his wife a look of gentle scolding.

'Oh, I do,' Rachel protested. 'I look for it but rarely find it.'

It was clear that the love between the rabbi and his wife did not stop them from disagreeing.

Rabbi Zimmerman was obviously uncomfortable with this conversation.

'Ronnie tries to stay away from the politics in the congregation,' Rachel continued. 'They try to drag him into it. Sometimes they tear him apart when there are two sparring teams on the board and each tries to get the rabbi on their side.'

'Rachel is cross with me because I didn't take sides when it came to Miki.'

Madison looked up at Rachel. The introduction of Miki into the conversation took him by surprise.

'Miki has been with the synagogue fifteen years,' Rachel said. 'People would tell you she put the synagogue on the map. Her work with the music in general and with the choir in particular was second to none. Every service, every concert under her baton brought glory to the synagogue. People came over from other synagogues. She was without a doubt the "queen" of this synagogue. And some people on the board – Cecil in particular – resented it.'

'Mr Kaufman?'

'Yes. And his dear wife, who, although not on the board, managed to run it through Cecil. I don't believe Cecil actually wanted to get rid of Miki. He wouldn't have wanted to be known as the one who did, but I am convinced that his wife pushed him to do it.'

‘Why?’

‘Well – with Miki – you love her or you hate her. Most of the congregation, I believe, loved her, but some really objected to her. The excellence of the singing, apparently, distracted them from praying. Speaking for myself, the wonderful singing in services helps me reach higher spheres of spirituality. It’s the bad singing that distracts me.’

The house phone rang at that moment and the rabbi answered.

‘Thank you, Miki,’ he said. ‘I will be over in a minute.’

He turned to face the other two.

‘They have arrived. I’m going over there. Would you like to come with me, Chief Inspector?’

Madison stood up.

‘I would, yes,’ he said. He turned to Rachel. ‘Thank you so much for a really lovely meal and for the interesting conversation,’ he said.

‘I hope I didn’t talk too much,’ Rachel said. ‘It’s my one failing. Once I get on my high horse, it’s difficult to restrain me.’

The rabbi smiled fondly at his wife.

‘You have only one failing?’ Madison asked, feigning astonishment.

‘She has many more,’ the rabbi said, giving his wife a gentle kiss on the cheek. ‘I’ll tell you all about it in the car.’

54

Sophie opened the door.

'Rabbi,' she said. 'Thank you so much for coming.'

'I brought the chief inspector with me, Sophie. I hope you don't mind.'

Sophie was taken aback for a second but immediately controlled herself.

'Chief Inspector,' she said. 'Please come in.'

She led the two men into the living room. Madison, as was his habit, studied the room and noted the same lack of care for the house as he'd detected in the garden. He found out often that people who in their work are meticulously clean and tidy are anything but in their own personal life.

As if reading his mind, Sophie said apologetically, 'My father wasn't "house proud". Had he known that people would be coming in and out of his house, I'm sure he would have taken care to—'

'That's absolutely fine, Sophie,' the rabbi said. 'It's not important.'

She pointed to two armchairs each side of the unlit fire and the two men sat down.

'Sophie, Rachel and I are so upset about your father. Please let us know if there is anything we can do. Help with the funeral, maybe?'

'Thanks, Rabbi. Father belonged to the local church here although, as you must realise, he spent more time in the synagogue than in the church.'

'Would you like me to talk to the minister? I have good relations with all the ministers in the area.'

Sophie smiled sadly.

'I might just take you up on it, Rabbi. I am still somewhat overwhelmed… and I would like you to say something at the funeral… if you are minded to do it.'

'Of course, I will, Sophie,' the rabbi replied. He looked around. 'I thought Miki was staying with you here?' he enquired.

'She is. She just nipped out to the shops. There is nothing in the house except a bit of milk and bread that are going off. I don't know how my dad lived like this…'

'Maybe he took food to the caravan,' the rabbi suggested.

'Yes, maybe…'

In the silence that followed, they could all hear the front door opening.

'That would be Miki,' Sophie said, and called out, 'Miki – in here.'

The living room door opened and Miki walked in.

'Hello, Rabbi,' she said, and then noticed Madison. The two men stood up.

'Chief Inspector,' she added, not daring to look at him, and hoping no one in the room noticed the colour in her face and her pulse racing.

'Can I get anyone a drink?' she said to the room at large.

The two men thanked her and declined.

'For goodness' sake, Miki – you have been fussing about from the moment we arrived. Just sit down. OK?'

Miki walked into the room and sat down next to Sophie.

'How are you, Miki?' the rabbi asked. 'We don't see much of you these days.'

'Sorry,' Miki replied. 'I just came back from a tour. Tell Rachel I will be in touch.'

'Sophie,' Madison interrupted. 'It would be easier if you two don't spend the night here.'

The room went quiet. Everyone was staring at Madison in a mixture of disbelief, worry and shock.

'I'm sorry. I don't wish to alarm you, but I would really rather you didn't stay here. Is there anywhere else you could stay?'

'What… what are you saying?' Sophie managed to say, trying to control herself. 'Are you saying we are… not safe here?'

Both the rabbi and Miki looked at him disapprovingly.

'I'm sorry,' Madison replied. 'I have been all around the houses with this case. I have looked at all the possibilities and investigated every hint, but I just can't dismiss the feeling I had from the start – that whoever killed Mr Kaufman came through this house and garden. Whoever did that has a key to this house, and, sadly, to the caravan also. I think that whoever did it feared that your father would eventually remember who he gave the key to, and they had to stop him. As long as this person is not caught, and as long as he or she still has the key to this house, I am not prepared to take any risks.'

The rabbi turned to Sophie.

'Sophie, you can come and stay with us tonight. Rachel would be delighted to have you.'

Sophie had given in to her emotions and was crying softly.

'If you prefer, Sophie, you can stay here and I will get an officer to stay with you.'

Sophie did not reply.

'I think that would be best,' Miki answered in her place, meeting Madison's eyes for the first time. 'Sophie has a room here with some of her clothes. She feels at home here.'

Madison stood up.

'That's settled, then,' he said. 'I will stay here until the officer arrives.'

Sophie looked up at Madison.

'That's why you asked me at the hospital if I had given anyone the keys to Dad's house.'

'Yes,' Madison replied. 'I had asked your father when I spoke to him and he was also adamant that he hadn't given the keys to anyone. Mr Adams – the neighbour – was also sure he never gave the key to anyone. And yet, somehow, someone has a key to this house.'

Madison took his phone out and moved towards the living room door.

'Chief Inspector,' Sophie said, and he turned to look at her. 'I'm sure this is nothing. It must be two or three years since… It was at that big concert you organised, Miki, with all the choirs. Dad left something at home… something they needed for the catering. He asked me to give her my keys so she could run to the house and bring what they needed. I didn't stay for the concert but she returned the keys to Dad the next day and he gave them back to me when I next came. I have the keys… right here.'

The silence in the room was heavy with the meaning of what she had just said.

'She?' Madison asked in a very soft, almost threatening voice. 'Who is she?'

55

Madison waited outside Jonson's house till the team arrived. Lisa, who lived closer, was the first to arrive.

'As of now, Jack,' she said, accusingly, 'I no longer have a boyfriend.'

'Lisa, I'm so sorry… you should have said.'

'That's fine, Jack. He wasn't really my type.'

Madison gave her a puzzled look.

'Why did you go out with him if he was not your type?'

'My types are all taken, or out of reach, or don't exist.'

She was not going to tell him that he was the one out of reach. Because he was out of reach.

Madison speedily updated her with the latest developments. Lisa listened, her eyes getting wider and wider.

'This is exciting!' she said when he finished. 'I wouldn't have missed it for the world.'

'Well.' Madison was quick to dampen her enthusiasm. 'I'm afraid I want you to stay here with the girls. Just in case she appears.'

'You think she would?'

'She certainly would intend to come, but maybe not tonight if she knows Miki is also here. How would she know, though? It was a last-minute decision. I don't think anyone knows that. However, she knows Sophie will be going back to London soon and she can't afford to wait. I'm not prepared to take a risk and I'm sure the two girls would rather have a woman officer.'

'Women,' Lisa said.

'What?'

'You referred to me as a woman but to them as "the girls". I think I'm younger than either of "the girls".'

'Are you telling me off again, Officer Thompson?'

Alarmed, Lisa looked up at Madison, but met the glint in his eye and relaxed.

'I wouldn't dare,' she said, and followed him inside the house.

Madison was serious this time. 'I'm sure you are more than a match for her.'

'You bet,' Lisa replied. 'I do amateur dramatics and I took a course in stage combat.'

'Stage combat? Have you not...?'

'I was joking, Jack. I took all the courses available. It's just that the stage combat looks so much better.'

They walked together into the house and Madison introduced Lisa.

'This is PC Thompson.'

'Lisa,' she corrected him, and immediately received grateful looks from Sophie and Miki.

'Yes – Lisa. She will make sure you are OK.'

'That's nice, Chief Inspector, but unnecessary,' Miki said. 'If she dares show her face here, I will know what to do!'

'I don't doubt that. Officer Thompson is here to protect *her*!'

Miki was wondering if Madison had really said what he did at the hospital. Could she have imagined it? His behaviour since gave no hint of the confession he made to her at the hospital.

'Why don't we all go in the kitchen and have a cup of tea?' Lisa suggested as soon as Madison left.

'How perfectly English!' Miki declared and led Lisa to the kitchen.

56

The three women were sitting at the little table in the kitchen, having some cheese and crackers – which Miki bought in the local shop – with a glass of red wine which Sophie found in her father's sideboard.

It was very clear to Lisa that Jon Jonson's life was not in this house. His life, she thought, was happening at the weekends, in the caravan with the woman he loved.

'I should have come here more often,' Sophie said. 'I can't believe this is how he lived. It wasn't like this when I came to visit. He must have made a special effort for my visits – which were not as often as they should have been.'

Lisa would have loved telling Sophie that Jon's life was full of love, if only at the weekends, but she did not think she had the authority to do so and, in any case, would Sophie be comforted or hurt by the fact that her father had led a life which he kept secret from her?

'There is no point in me telling you not to feel guilty, Sophie,' Miki said. 'Because you still will. I lost my father and my mother and, in both cases, I felt guilty as hell. I still do. I honestly believe that every death leaves behind a ton of guilt. You can't live your life thinking every day that you must be nice to a person you might lose. It's part of the mourning, so don't fight it. Let it happen and, eventually, you will learn to live with it.'

'Lisa,' Sophie said. 'You are making me nervous.'

Lisa was standing by the kitchen window, wine glass in hand, looking out on the dark garden.

'Sorry,' Lisa said, and came back to the table.

'You don't really think she can get into the garden, do you?' Sophie was looking for a reassuring answer. 'The only way into the garden is through the house,' she added. Lisa did not want to alarm the two women but thought that, if the woman had copies of Jon's keys, she must also have the key to the synagogue, and therefore to the Jonsons' garden.

She looked up to find Miki's eyes fixed on her. Miki replied to the unspoken concern Lisa had.

'Even if she has a key to the synagogue,' Miki said, 'the alarm would go off until she went inside the building and switched it off. We would hear the alarm.'

'Ignore me,' Lisa said. 'I am on duty so I have to be seen to be working.'

The three women smiled as they allowed themselves to relax a little.

'Do you miss working at the synagogue?' Lisa asked, cutting herself another chunk of cheese.

'If I'm honest,' Miki replied, 'not really. Not the work. So many years of my life were spent trying to do a professional job with a group of people, none of whom were professional musicians. Although it is satisfying to succeed in almost getting them to sound like a professional group, it takes so much more time and effort. No – I think I have done enough of that. But I do miss the people. Rather – some people.'

'My father liked the rabbi and his wife,' Sophie said.

'Yes, I like them too. They are friends, so I haven't lost them,' Miki said. 'Particularly Rachel. We have become very close.'

Lisa stood up.

'I won't be a minute,' she said, and walked out of the kitchen. Although she was trying to put the women's minds at rest, she was restless. She walked around the rooms downstairs, looked through the window in the lounge – she could see nothing in the garden. She climbed the stairs quickly and checked every room – just in case. Madison trusted her with the safety of these women and she was going to do her damnedest to protect them.

She walked back into the kitchen.

Sophie and Lisa were deep in conversation and she sat back at the table almost unnoticed.

'How he ever got to qualify as a rabbi is beyond comprehension,' Miki said.

'Rabbi Zimmerman?' Lisa asked, a little surprised.

Miki laughed.

'No. Not Ronnie. Ronnie is everything that the previous rabbi wasn't. For a start, he is very knowledgeable. The previous one was useless. He knew so little about the services and the tradition that he needed to get advice from members of the synagogue. On top of that he was really lazy, always looking for people to take bits of his job off him. And the worst – no charisma. No inspiration. I used to fall asleep by the piano during his sermons.'

The three women laughed at the image of this energetic woman being put to sleep by a dull sermon.

And then the doorbell rang.

The three women froze.

After a moment, Sophie said, 'It must be the chief inspector.' She got up and started moving towards the door.

Lisa stopped her.

'It is not the chief inspector,' she said. 'Madison would not ring the doorbell. He would call me.'

57

The journey passed in silence. Madison and Brodmann – the more experienced officers – were pondering on the fact that they had never before encountered such an unusual criminal. In fact, in the face of all the evidence – the keys, the opportunity – they were not absolutely certain they had their man – or in this case, their woman. This investigation had led them in different directions, and each one proved to be false. Could this one also lead to nothing?

Benson, on the other hand, was quietly excited. This would be his first time apprehending a criminal. It was obviously not going to be a dangerous, professional criminal but, as a first time, it would do. He could not wait.

Madison parked his Yeti down the road, so it could not be seen from the house.

'Josh,' he said softly as they were making their way up to the house, 'you go around the back to make sure she doesn't escape through the garden. Dave – you come with me.'

Josh disappeared into the darkness. Madison gave him a moment or two to arrive at the back of the house and then pressed the doorbell.

'No car in the drive,' Brodmann commented.

Madison pressed the bell again.

'The drive goes around to the back. She could have parked at the back.'

Brodmann disappeared into the darkness of the back garden and returned.

'No car,' he said.

Madison rang the doorbell again.

And again – nothing happened.

'Damn!' Madison said under his breath. 'I was hoping to catch her at home.'

He took out his mobile phone and dialled Lisa's number.

'Lisa?' he said, then paused. 'Hello? Who is it? Sophie? Why? Where is Lisa?'

58

The three women remained sitting, as if frozen. Then Lisa stood up.

'I'm going to see who it is,' she said, starting towards the door.

'I'm coming with you,' Miki said, and stood up.

'No, you're not,' Lisa said firmly. 'You stay here with Sophie.'

'It could be Mr Adams,' Sophie said without conviction. 'The neighbour. He said he would call in on me.'

'At ten thirty at night?' Lisa dismissed the suggestion. 'Please stay here.'

Lisa closed the kitchen door after her and moved towards the front door.

She looked through the peephole but saw no one.

'Kids having fun,' she said to herself while opening the door.

She could see no one. She came down the front steps, which was when she saw her.

'Mrs Kaufman!' she said, obviously surprised.

Mrs Kaufman moved out of the shadows into the light streaming out from the hallway.

'You!' she said with obvious displeasure. 'What are you doing here?'

'I was about to ask you the same question,' Lisa replied.

'I came to see Sophie. Is she here?'

'Sophie is not seeing people,' Lisa replied, weighing her options.

'I made her a casserole,' Mrs Kaufman said.

She took a Pyrex dish out of a carrying bag.

'You probably don't know it,' she said with contempt, 'but this is what we do when we visit a house of mourning.'

Lisa was debating with herself her next move. Should she arrest Mrs Kaufman on the doorstep? She did not fancy doing that outside where the woman could escape easily before she got hold of her. Better to get her inside the house.

'You'd better bring it in then, Mrs Kaufman,' Lisa said.

She turned around and walked towards the first step when, suddenly, something hit her on the head and she dropped down on the steps, hitting her head again.

59

Miki and Sophie heard Lisa's cry as she fell.

Miki ran to the door and Sophie followed behind her. They saw Lisa sprawled over the two steps to the front door and Mrs Kaufman, a casserole dish in her hand, stepping over Lisa and walking into the house.

Mrs Kaufman stopped when she saw Miki.

'Well, well, well,' she exclaimed. 'The queen herself.'

'What have you done?' Miki shouted at her and rushed over to Lisa, who was still lying in the doorway, not moving.

Mrs Kaufman moved to block Miki's way. She dropped the Pyrex dish on the floor, which distracted Miki for a moment, long enough for Mrs Kaufman to lift her hand high and bring it down on Miki.

Miki saw the movement and managed to move her head just in time, but the hand landed on her upper arm with such force Miki let out a shout of pain. This made Sophie rush to her, and caused Lisa to finally start moving.

Miki would later say that she did not know she was capable of such violence. She lunged at Mrs Kaufman with force she did not know she possessed. She boxed the older woman in her face – another thing she had never done before – with such power she knocked her to the ground. She then jumped on Mrs Kaufman, twisting her arm till the woman screamed and let go of the object she was holding. It was a little heavy figurine. Miki threw it far away and heard it crack. Mrs Kaufman tried to get up but Miki was stronger and much angrier. She hit her again and again and continued even when Mrs Kaufman stopped moving.

'Miki!' Sophie called out to her. 'Stop! Enough. You are killing her!'

Miki stopped but remained sitting on the woman.

'We need to tie her up,' she said softly. 'Do you think you can find something…'

'Here,' Lisa whispered as she was coming to. 'Take these.'

She reached into her deep pocket and took out her handcuffs.

Sophie took the cuffs from Lisa and cuffed Mrs Kaufman's wrists.

At that moment, Lisa's phone rang. Lisa started moving to answer it but everything was going around and she could not focus her eyes.

Sophie took Lisa's phone and answered the call.

'Lisa?' She heard Madison's voice on the phone.

'No, it's Sophie.'

'Sophie?' Madison's voice became louder. 'Why? Where is Lisa?'

When on duty, Madison expected his officers to take their phones with them at all times – even when relieving themselves.

'Well… she is here… but…'

'I'm OK.' Lisa tried speaking louder.

'She says she is OK,' Sophie reported, sounding doubtful.

'What happened?' Madison was clearly anxious. 'Where is Miki?'

'Well… she is kind of busy. She is… sitting on Mrs Kaufman.'

The phone went quiet. Sophie just realised how stupid she sounded and started laughing. At first hesitantly but then louder and louder, till she was screaming with laughter.

Sophie was getting more hysterical by the moment and Miki called out to her, getting louder and louder.

'Sophie!' she shouted. 'Sophie! Sophie!'

She kept calling Sophie's name till the laughter stopped. It was replaced by a soft, pitiful crying.

60

Madison put his foot down and drove well above the speed limit.

'I should never have left Lisa alone with them,' Madison said.

'Easy on the pedal, Jack!' Brodmann said. 'It won't help anyone if we have an accident now.'

'Put the siren on,' Madison said and Brodmann obeyed. He placed the lights on top of the car and started the siren going. With the siren screaming away, Madison increased the speed.

'I will never forgive myself,' he mumbled.

'Jack!' Brodmann said. 'Lisa is a police officer. There was no reason to think that she could not deal with the woman.'

Madison did not reply. He concentrated on his driving.

No one said anything and, for the rest of the drive, only the police siren could be heard.

61

The officers burst through the open door and took in the picture.

In the middle of the hallway, Miki was sitting on Mrs Kaufman, who was now awake, cursing, throwing her cuffed hands in the air and trying to push Miki off her. Lisa was sitting on the floor, leaning against the wall, hand on her head, trying to recover, and Sophie was holding a glass of water, making Lisa drink.

'Dave,' Madison said, pointing at Mrs Kaufman, 'sort her out.'

He then joined Sophie, kneeling by Lisa.

'Lisa – can you hear me?' he said in a very loud voice.

'Of course, I can hear you,' she answered. 'There's no need to shout. I have a dreadful headache.'

In the background they could hear Brodmann reading Mrs Kaufman her rights while Benson was helping her off the ground and holding her firmly.

'I'm taking you to hospital,' Madison said, and started helping Lisa up.

'There is no need,' Lisa said. 'It's just a headache.'

'I am taking you to the hospital!' Madison repeated. 'No arguments. Dave – can I leave you two to finish here?'

'Of course,' Dave said, holding up the broken figurine. 'Miki had disarmed her so I don't foresee any problems.'

'I'm sorry, Jack. I let you down,' Lisa managed to say.

'You can tell me all about it in the car,' Madison said.

Leaning on Madison on one side and Sophie on the other, Lisa slowly made her way towards Madison's car.

'She caught me completely by surprise,' Lisa murmured as she settled in the passenger seat.

'She caught us all by surprise,' Madison answered as he got into the driver's seat.

He started the engine and was about to close the driver's door when Sophie said, 'Miki is also hurt.'

'What?' Madison turned off the engine.

'I think she missed. She was aiming at her head also, but Miki ducked and she got her on her shoulder or back.'

'Sophie, can you stay here with Lisa?' Madison said and, not waiting for her reply, rushed back into the house.

They were all still in the hall. Miki was sitting down, watching the officers arresting Mrs Kaufman, who had stopped shouting and was now perfectly silent.

'Miki,' Madison said sternly. 'You are also hurt?'

'I am OK,' she answered, fighting the tears that were threatening to betray her stupid reaction to the care in his voice. 'It's just my shoulder… nothing really.'

'I would rather a doctor checked you out,' Madison insisted.

'No,' Miki said determinedly. 'I'm fine.'

She spoke without looking at Madison, still fighting the emotional state she was in. She was beginning to realise quite how much the last hour took out of her.

Madison hesitated for a minute, then turned around and went back to the car.

He drove in silence for a while and it took him time to realise that Lisa was crying softly.

'Lisa, are you OK?'

'I'm fine,' she said again. 'I'm fine.'

'Are you in pain? I could put the siren on and get you there faster.'

'No!' She raised her voice and regretted it immediately as the pain shot through her head. 'I'm… I let you all down. An old, pathetic woman and she got me… I will… I will hand in my resignation letter as soon as I'm back.'

Madison stopped the car suddenly and turned to face her.

'Lisa, if every time a police officer gets it wrong, he or she resigns, there will be no officers. We all make mistakes. It is a lot more my mistake than yours. The woman was so nasty, so unpleasant, so hateful that she completely fooled us. Even when it was clear she must have committed the murders, I would never have thought her dangerous in a one-to-one with a police officer. You are a good officer. You will learn from this and become an even better one. Now – let's concentrate on getting you better so you can resume your duties.'

Madison turned back to look at the road and started the car.

62

DAY 15

'The date is twenty-first of March. The time is eleven am. Present are DCI Jack Madison and Sergeant Brodmann. Also present, Mrs Linda Kaufman. Mrs Kaufman,' Madison continued, 'are you sure you do not wish to have a solicitor present?'

Mrs Kaufman stared at Madison and did not reply.

'Or someone to support you?'

Mrs Kaufman gave Madison a blood-curdling stare.

'I have all the support I need.' She practically spat the words at him. 'I have Sergeant Brodmann here.'

Both officers were taken aback at this.

'I'm afraid that is not how it works, Mrs Kaufman,' Madison said. 'The sergeant is here to question you, not to support you.'

Mrs Kaufman turned her chair so she was practically giving Madison her back and facing Brodmann.

Madison spoke to the tape. 'Mrs Kaufman refuses a solicitor or anyone else.'

Mrs Kaufman's arm was strapped and held in a sling. Miki clearly did real damage to her arm.

There was no response from Mrs Kaufman, and Madison continued.

'We have searched your bag and the house but we can't find them. Where have you hidden them?'

Mrs Kaufman briefly glanced at Madison.

'Hidden what?' she asked.

'The keys, Mrs Kaufman. The keys to Mr Jonson's house and caravan.'

Mrs Kaufman turned her back on Madison again and did not reply.

Madison gave Brodmann a meaningful look and Brodmann, reluctantly, took over.

'Mrs Kaufman,' he started, but she stopped him immediately.

'YOU,' she said, emphasising the word, 'you can call me Linda.'

Brodmann glanced at Madison, who nodded his approval. With a tortured look on his face, Brodmann turned back to Mrs Kaufman.

'Linda,' he said. 'I don't understand. Why? Why did you do it?'

'*Mr* Brodmann,' she said, emphasising the mister. 'Are you married?'

Brodmann knew he should be deflecting this question, but he also knew that this was his only chance of getting her to open up.

'I am, yes.'

'Is your wife happy?'

Brodmann wished he was somewhere else. Anywhere, but talking to this woman.

'I hope so,' he said softly, aware of Madison watching him. He knew that Madison would be amused by his difficulty with this woman and it made him angry.

'Is she proud of you, Mr Brodmann?' Again, she put emphasis on the use of mister instead of sergeant.

'I really wouldn't know, Mrs Kaufman, and I really think we should not be talking about—'

'If she is proud of you, she is happy, Mr Brodmann.'

A short silence followed.

'Why do you say that, Mrs Kaufman?' Brodmann asked carefully.

'Can I please have a glass of water?' she asked, taking Brodmann by surprise, again. He had never before met a person who could so easily throw him out of his comfort zone.

'Of course,' Brodmann answered, and started getting up. Madison stopped him and walked out of the room himself. The chief inspector going out to get a suspect a glass of water? Brodmann thought he should be enjoying this moment, but he really was not.

After a short pause, she continued.

'If a woman can't be proud of her husband,' she said, 'she can't be happy. Can she?'

Brodmann spoke slowly and carefully.

'And you were not happy?'

Mrs Kaufman looked away from Brodmann and stared through the little window, through which one could see another wing of the police station and just a hint of sky. When she spoke, she seemed to be speaking to no one in particular.

'I tried so hard. I got him the job down south with this firm. The boss knew my father. Reputable accountants. Cecil was an accountant, you know? I kept him while he studied to be an accountant. There were times I thought he would never do it but, in the end, he qualified. He joined that firm and it was so obvious they were not pleased. I did everything I could. I organised parties, I invited people to dinner – you could tell that even when they came, they really did that because they could not say no. To me. Eventually, he was fired.

'I belong in the south of England. I never wanted to come up north, but once he lost his job, we couldn't afford to keep the house. We sold and moved up here.'

She stopped talking when Madison walked back into the room with a glass of water. He placed the glass in front of her. She looked at the glass for a few seconds, as if debating whether she should be drinking it or not, but in the end she reached for the glass and had a long drink.

The two officers remained silent, watching her drink.

'It wasn't any better up here,' she said, turning again to face Brodmann. 'He couldn't get a job. Had some freelance work but nothing more. We were eating into my inheritance. I didn't want to join this synagogue. I wanted to join a real synagogue. You know what I mean, Mr Brodmann, don't you?'

Brodmann did not need to look at Madison to know he was enjoying this 'camaraderie' between himself and Mrs Kaufman. Reluctantly, he nodded his agreement to her.

'But he wanted to be the chair of the board and he would have no chance at the Orthodox synagogue. They were all doctors and solicitors and such like in that one, so we joined this synagogue, and after a lot of hard work on my part, we finally managed to get him on the board. When he offered himself to be the chair, he almost didn't get it. There were a lot of objections, which apparently is unheard of, but finally he made it. Finally, he achieved something I could be proud of him for.'

She stopped again to have a drink of water. Madison and Brodmann exchanged a look – Brodmann's filled with resentment, and Madison's a part-amused, part-encouraging look.

Brodmann turned back to look at Mrs Kaufman and she returned his look eagerly, sitting a little forwards in her seat, as if trying to get closer to him.

'And then he lost it,' she said. 'All because of that bitch, Miki Solomon.'

There was so much venom in the sentence Brodmann felt as if he had been hit in the face.

'Miki?' he asked. 'What did she do?'

'She fought him from the moment he became chair. There were some complaints against her… There always were, but in the past the board preferred to ignore them because they wanted to keep her. Cecil took the complaints seriously. After all, this was supposed to be a synagogue, not an opera house with a prima donna ruling over it. It didn't matter how many people complained… the chair has to deal with every complaint, and these were two important members of the synagogue. She refused to even refer to it, and instead went and resigned.'

'You didn't want her to resign?'

'I would have preferred her to be sacked. But apparently this congregation, who don't know what's good for them, didn't want her to go, and instead voted Cecil off the board.'

Mrs Kaufman took another sip of her water. To Brodmann's relief, she did not need any more prompting. It was almost as if once she started rolling the ball down the hill, she could not stop it.

'I didn't know what more I could do,' she said. 'I couldn't see where else to go. It was all too humiliating. Everyone knew he was voted off. You see – I had some hope that through his chairmanship he might be offered some work, but now that everyone knew he had been sacked even from this position, there was no hope. There was nowhere to move to. We had already escaped from the south. How much lower could we go? And I did not want to burn all my inheritance on this useless man I married. There was just enough to keep me for the rest of my life. Not both of us.'

At this point, Madison interfered.

'So that's why you killed him?' he enquired.

'Yes, Chief Inspector.' She spat the venom in his direction. 'That's why I killed him and I do not regret it. I have had enough!'

'But why not just divorce him?'

'Divorce? Who do you think I am? How much disgrace do you think I can bring on myself and my family?'

The irony is clearly lost on her, Madison thought. *Is being divorced a worse disgrace than being a murderer?*

Madison moved closer to the table and softened his voice, while staring right at her.

'Mrs Kaufman,' he started. 'You had us fooled. How did you do it?'

Mrs Kaufman returned his look. She was clearly not flattered by his attempt to compliment her, but she was tired. She knew she had lost the battle. She had been found out and there was no point pretending otherwise.

'I think you know how,' she said without emotion.

'You had the keys to Mr Jonson's house. Right?'

'I have always been a very useful kind of a person. Never miss a chance to do something useful,' she said, flatly. 'If I think something might be useful in the future, I keep it. So, when Jonson asked his daughter to give me the key to his house so I could get something he left behind, I made copies of all the keys on his key ring.'

She smiled, almost in pride.

'I have the keys to the synagogue also. And the keys to his daughter's house in London. On the off chance...'

There was a moment of silence while Brodmann was hoping Madison was taking over the questioning, and Madison was thinking how to proceed without closing this narrow window that opened up.

'How did you know your husband was going to be up on the balcony in the synagogue?' he asked finally.

'How did I know?' She said this with contempt. 'I didn't KNOW! I made sure. I asked Cecil to get something from the choir cupboard up in the balcony. A book I lent someone who left it in that cupboard. As a matter of fact, I had already removed the book from there, so I knew he would be there a while, looking for it. I watched from downstairs until I knew he was where I wanted him to be.'

'We never found the object he was hit with. I guess it was the same little figurine you hit my officer with?'

Mrs Kaufman smiled.

'It was my lucky mascot,' she said. 'It never let me down. It used to be my mother's. I could aways count on this little angel,' she added, and then her face turned red with hatred. 'That is, until Miki broke it. Unforgivable.'

Madison and Brodmann exchanged a look of bewilderment.

'Your lucky mascot?' Brodmann found the words first. 'You have… used it before?'

'Many times,' Mrs Kaufman replied with a victorious little smile.

'You… hit people with this little figurine?'

'Not people,' she replied, deep in thought. 'No. Cecil was the first. No. I used it on my cats… and one dog… and I always returned it to the mantelpiece and no one suspected. In fact, it was standing on top of my fireplace, right in front of your face when you came to talk to me. And you never guessed.'

She stopped talking while the two officers were slowly coming to the realisation that they were dealing with a dangerous psychopath under the guise of a little old lady.

Mrs Kaufman remained deep in her thoughts, and when she spoke again, it was as if she had forgotten the two officers in the room, and she was talking to herself.

'My mother bought the little figure many years ago in Jerusalem. It is the Wailing Wall – the western wall of the temple that was destroyed. It has the prayer of the road written over the stones. I thought it was really appropriate, as I was sending him on his way. It is quite small. Fitted very well in my handbag – but it is very heavy and it has sharp corners. When Cecil saw me up in the balcony he was surprised. But he didn't know I came through Jon's house. I said I wasn't sure he would remember so I came up to fetch the book myself. As he turned his back to me, I hit him hard with the statuette. He never knew what hit him. I thought of it as a mercy killing.'

Madison knew the answer to the next question but asked it nevertheless.

'Why Jonson, though? What did Jonson do?'

Mrs Kaufman shook her head, as if waking from a dream, and looked at Madison with naked hatred.

'You are supposed to be a detective.' Mrs Kaufman threw the words at him with scorn. 'You work it out.'

Madison threw a quick glance at Brodmann and motioned him to take over. Mrs Kaufman was getting negative again and Madison wanted a full confession, recorded and served at her trial.

Brodmann also knew the answer to the question. He moved forwards on his chair and spoke softly and intimately.

'Because you thought he would sooner or later remember the keys?'

She turned to look at Brodmann with relief.

'You understand. Don't you?'

'I understand. Yes,' Brodmann replied. The words stuck in his throat and he thought he might vomit.

'I got away with it,' Mrs Kaufman said. 'I was finally living the life I wanted to live. No money worries, no debts. My money was my own and I could do what I wanted with it. I booked a holiday to New York. I always wanted to visit New

York. I had tasted freedom at last, and I didn't want to give it up. At least not so soon. Jonson – not the brightest bulb in the universe – would have eventually remembered about the keys. I saw to it that he couldn't.'

Mrs Kaufman stopped and took a sip of water. It was a relief to talk. Since Cecil died she had no one to talk to from one day to the next. She missed talking, even though she knew that most of the time Cecil just tolerated her talking and did not really listen. Here were two officers, and they were listening to every word she said very attentively. Mrs Kaufman had never before had such a willing audience.

'I knew Mr Jonson drove to his caravan every Sunday afternoon, after he locked the synagogue for the day. So, I drove there Saturday night, late. Made sure no one saw me. I let myself in, turned the gas on and left. It couldn't have taken more than three minutes. I wasn't sure it would work. I would've preferred to use the figurine again but I didn't see how I could. So, it had to be the caravan. I didn't know how much gas there was in the tank but I figured even if it ran out before he came, the caravan should still have plenty of gas in the air. All the windows were closed. I couldn't let this nobody floor washer destroy me.'

Madison had his confession. He no longer worried about antagonising her.

'But his daughter also knew. Didn't she?' Madison's tone was challenging.

'Yes, she did,' Mrs Kaufman confirmed. 'I guess she told you? I was too late with her. I knew she would come up for his funeral. I should have dealt with her sooner.'

Madison stood up.

'There is just one more thing I don't understand, Mrs Kaufman,' Brodmann said, standing up too. 'Where are your keys? We checked your bag and your car – we can't find them.'

Mrs Kaufman smiled arrogantly.

'Ah, my keys! My special keys. I had the rabbi's house keys also. And some members of the board.'

Brodmann was still curious.

'So where are they now?' he asked, not really expecting a reply. They would have to search the garden, the street, just in case she managed to open the window without anyone noticing. He was not looking forward to it.

'Wouldn't you like to know, Sergeant,' she said daringly.

'I would, yes,' he replied.

'Well, if you were a woman, Sergeant, you would probably know,' she said, almost laughing.

Brodmann pondered that remark. It rang a bell. He thought for a few minutes and then a smile appeared on his face.

'Gov,' he said, keeping his eyes on Mrs Kaufman, 'can we get a woman officer in here? We will need to do a body search.'

For once, Madison was lost.

'A body search?'

'Angi sometimes does that when she wants to keep her hands free.'

'Does what?' Madison was getting frustrated.

'Keeps things in her bra,' Brodmann said, staring at the appropriate section of Mrs Kaufman's front.

Madison got it.

'I see,' he said. 'Should I bring in a woman officer to search you, or will you give us the keys?'

Mrs Kaufman held the chief inspector's eyes for a while, and then started laughing aloud. It was a weird, scary laughter.

'Mr Chief Inspector, why don't you come and get it, if you dare?'

Madison returned her look and for a while they were staring at each other, her laughing louder and louder and him looking sterner by the moment.

'I do, Mrs Kaufman. I do dare,' he said, and moved towards her.

Brodmann tried to stop him.

'Come on, Jack,' he said, but Madison pushed him aside and moved closer to Mrs Kaufman.

Mrs Kaufman could see that Madison meant business. She stopped laughing and, still looking at him, lifted her arm, dramatically, then put it unceremoniously inside her bra, and brought her hand out holding the key ring, with keys galore dangling off it. She moved it about and the room was filled with the metallic sound of keys crashing against each other.

She turned away from Madison and handed them to Brodmann.

'It was damned uncomfortable,' she announced.

'Book her!' Madison said and stood up. He needed some fresh air.

'Chief Inspector Madison is leaving the room,' Brodmann said to the tape.

63

DAY 16

The four officers attended the funeral of Jon Jonson.

Brodmann did not go in for the service.

'I know you will laugh at me,' he said to Madison, 'but I can't. It's been drilled into me from early age. Jews don't go into churches.'

'What if we were called to a murder in a church. You would not go in?'

'That would be different. It would be my job. It wouldn't be going to attend a service.'

'I am amazed,' Madison said. 'The church is almost full. Mostly with Jewish people. How come they can go and you can't?'

'You know the answer to that.'

'I know. They are not real Jews.'

'I didn't say that. They are just not my kind of Jews.'

'Hitler would have considered them all proper Jews. Just like you.'

'Enough, Jack. Just stop it.'

Madison smiled and walked away from Brodmann, who waited outside.

Before the service, Sophie spoke to Rabbi Zimmerman.

'Rabbi,' she said, 'my father told me how moved he always was when attending a funeral in your congregation, when a member of the family read the special prayer. I can't remember what it was called.'

'The Kaddish,' the rabbi said.

'I know he wasn't Jewish, but is there any way that you can read this prayer at the graveside?'

'I don't think I can, sorry, Sophie,' the rabbi replied. 'But I think you can ask someone else to read it for you? Half my congregation is here and they would not appreciate the rabbi doing this, but if you can find someone who has no such boundaries…'

'Miki will do it,' Sophie said. 'I'm sure she will. Would that be OK with you?'

'Sure. If Miki agrees to do it, it would be fine with me.'

Miki did not hesitate for a minute.

'As you know, Sophie,' Miki said, 'I don't hold with all these rules and regulations. If you want me to read it, I will. Jon was what we call "an honorary Jew". He was one of us.'

'Thanks,' Sophie said. 'I am sure Dad would have loved it to be read by you. He really liked you.'

'It's settled then,' Miki said.

It was a short service. The minister gave the podium to Rabbi Zimmerman, who spoke fondly of Jon Jonson and his devoted service to the Jewish congregation of Beit Chaverim.

Sophie just about controlled her emotions when she spoke about her father and what he meant to her. Many people were tearful. Jonson was liked by all and the manner in which he died shocked and upset everyone.

As they all left the church, Brodmann joined the procession on its way to the grave.

He walked with the other officers, all four wearing their uniform as a sign of respect.

As they reached the grave, Sophie and Miki stood together. The four officers stood on the other side of the grave opposite them. Miki suddenly felt nervous. She tried to avoid looking at Madison but could not help glance at him occasionally. Every glance met his steady and fixed gaze.

She suddenly felt self-conscious, which was not like her, and found herself wishing she had not promised to do the Kaddish.

But the time came and the minister gave her a sign. She opened the prayer book and, in a voice which was not as steady as she would have expected of herself, she started reading the Kaddish.

'*Yitgadal ve'yitkadash Shmei Raba…*'

The people gathered were silent as her voice, reading the familiar prayer but in the rarely heard Israeli accent, rang around the cemetery.

Miki was angry with herself, as she was very aware of Madison watching her and she felt she should be thinking of Jonson, who she liked and who could never do enough for her. She felt she was letting Sophie down, but would make sure Sophie would never know.

When it was over, people filed by Sophie and stopped to shake her hand and murmur their sympathies.

The difference between how this congregation mourned with Sophie and the awkward way they tried to support Mrs Kaufman was obvious.

The officers followed suit, said a few words and moved on. When it was Madison's turn, he took Sophie's hand, expressed his condolences and gave her his best wishes.

'I want to thank you, Chief Inspector,' she said warmly.

'I have to thank you, Sophie. If not for you we would not have solved the case.'

'But I had this information the whole time. If only I had

told you sooner, you might have… my father might still be alive.'

'Don't beat yourself up about it,' Madison replied. 'It was such a long time ago… your father also had the information, and never remembered it. You have to put this out of your mind. I am sure he would not want you to blame yourself.'

'I know,' she said softly. The tears had dried up. 'It will be very difficult to go into the house again. I will always see her walking into the house, with the little figurine in her hands…'

'Are you staying with Miki tonight?' Madison asked.

'No. I am driving straight from here to London. I can't get out of here fast enough. The house belongs to the synagogue, so thankfully I don't have to sell it. I have taken things that I want to keep, and the rest – the rabbi promised they would engage a house clearing company… I don't ever want to see that place again.'

Madison walked away, bowing his head to acknowledge Miki, but moving away without a word.

As she was leaving the synagogue, Miki felt her stomach twist with frustration, nerves and anger. Did he really say what he did at the hospital? Was he playing with her? Why was she letting it get to her?

She promised herself she would do her best to forget him.

64

The team gathered in their little incident room. Madison got some champagne – or at least quality fizzy white wine – and they all celebrated the successful conclusion to the case.

They helped Benson dismantle the room and return it to its former existence as the caretaker's room. The caretaker was gone and they all felt frustration that they did not stop his killing.

'If only Jonson told me when I was questioning him,' Brodmann said. 'If only he'd remembered—'

'We are not doing this, Dave!' Madison interrupted him. 'This is not the first time we've lost people because we solved a case too late. If we can't live with it, we can't do the job. Try to think of the fact that we saved Sophie. One or two more days and she would have got to Sophie, too.'

'You were right from the start, Jack,' Lisa said. 'You said from the start that it was to do with Jonson's house and the keys.'

'Not from the start, unfortunately. Only from the moment I found out that Jonson's garden opened up into the synagogue grounds. You could say that if I was quicker with that, we could have saved Jonson. I try not to torture myself with these ifs. That's what we have – and on to the next case.'

They helped Benson carry the kettle, cups, sugar and the like to his car.

'Pub?' Dave asked.

The two young officers replied with enthusiasm.

Madison put his hand in his pocket and got out a twenty-pound note.

'Have your drinks on me,' he said, and handed Dave the money. 'I have plans.'

Dave looked at Madison and almost said something, but decided against it. He knew his friend well and the look in Madison's eyes told him to keep well off the subject.

Madison left the team and walked to the Yeti that was patiently waiting for him in the synagogue's car park.

65

After bidding Sophie farewell, Miki drove home. She loved her little home and she valued her independence. It was good to be home again, and alone.

She had a long shower, put on her cosy, fluffy robe and settled on her sofa, trying to listen to the trio's latest recording.

But the familiar feeling of comfort she expected in her own space was not coming. There was a knot in her stomach which she was trying to ignore, to no avail. She found it hard to concentrate on the music and found sitting on her wonderful sofa restless. She got off the sofa and went to make herself a drink.

While the kettle was boiling, she walked up and down her kitchen – a routine that proved useful in the past when she was feeling nervous before a concert.

It did not work. The knot in her stomach was getting so tight it almost hurt.

She was angry. Mostly with herself. How could she allow herself to get into this state. About a man?

Miki had had men in her life since the 'forbidden love'. She enjoyed men's company and occasionally engaged in more intimate relationships, but these were always on her terms. She engaged when it pleased her and removed herself when it no longer pleased her.

Why did he speak to her at the hospital? Why did he say what he said? He left her in turmoil from which she was yet to recover. She thought he would follow it at the cemetery, when it was obvious the case was over and he was never coming back. She thought he would discreetly ask for her phone number. Email address. She was not prepared for him to walk past her and disappear.

Had he not said what he did at the hospital, maybe she could forget him, although she'd felt a strong pull towards him almost from the start. Why did he feel it was necessary to say what he did to her? A simple apology for his behaviour would have been enough.

She took her drink back in the living room but could not settle down. She discarded the recording and, instead, chose Brahms's second symphony. She glanced at the clock – the time was nine thirty. She had never had any complaints from her neighbours, but she was always strict with keeping the sound low after ten in the evening. She put the volume high and walked around the room, listening to the haunting music. She had half an hour to calm down before the volume would have to be taken down.

She moved around the room, swaying with the music, singing the most dramatic bits in a tortured, almost tearful tone.

The Brahms was playing so loud that at first she did not hear the doorbell.

She stopped moving and turned the sound down. She listened and there it was again. The doorbell.

It was nine thirty-four in the evening. Late for any casual callers. She was in her robe. She was not sure she should open the door.

Her heart was beating loudly as she walked hesitantly towards the door.

She opened the door to reveal Madison standing there, practically filling the door frame.

'You should have a chain on the door,' he said and then, moving fast, he walked in, slammed the door shut behind him and grabbed Miki in his arms.

Before she could utter a sound, they were kissing, and he held her so tightly to his chest that she could not tell if the beating in her ears was her heartbeat or his.

After eternity, she pulled away to take some air while still held tightly in his arms.

'Jack,' she managed to whisper.

He stopped her.

'You can call me Chief Inspector,' he said as his face broke into a gigantic smile.

Her heart missed a beat. She realised that she had fallen in love with a man she had never before seen smiling. The smile transformed his face in a way she had never seen before. It stretched from ear to ear; his eyes were dancing; even the structure of his face suddenly seemed different. His cheekbones were protruding, his eyebrows, always so severe and threatening, turned into two soft, rounded arches laughing with his eyes.

Miki watched this transformation with fascination.

'You should smile more often,' she said, still struggling to find her voice. 'You have no idea…'

The smile widened further.

'Oh, I do. I do have an idea. That is why I use it so guardedly.'

'Arrogant bastard,' she said, this time aloud.

He drew her close again and kissed her more gently.

When she caught her breath again, she asked, 'Are we going to stay in the hallway all night or would you like to come in?'

Madison released her.

'Before we go any further,' he said, 'I need to ask you a question.'

She tensed up.

'I thought the case was over?'

'It is nothing to do with the case,' he replied. 'It is to do with your "forbidden love". I need to know if it is over. I don't play second fiddle to anyone.'

'That's funny,' she replied, teasingly. 'I play second fiddle quite often.'

She looked up at Madison and noted that the magical smile was no more. He was fixing her with the gaze she was now familiar with.

'I think it has been over for years,' she replied. 'The fact that we hadn't met in all this time kept it open when it was really shut. I met him in Amsterdam during the last tour. It was no longer forbidden. We were free to love, but didn't. I sometimes wonder if it was the "forbidden" element that was so enticing. In a way I will always love him because he was part of my life. But not in that way.'

Madison watched her for a while, as if deciding how genuine her answer was.

'This will do for now,' he said at last. 'In time, I will need to know more about it, but for now, I just want you.'

Miki relaxed and smiled.

'I am all yours, Chief Inspector.'

And she melted into his arms.

END

ACKNOWLEDGEMENTS

I would like to thank Andrew Curry and David Spencer for their invaluable help with police procedures.

Many thanks to my good friend Morag Sanig for reading and proofreading the book, and for her encouragement.

And last but most definitely not least, my husband Peter, for his belief in me, his support and for checking every word I ever wrote in English. Without you, I simply couldn't do it.